THE MURDER OF GIANNI VERSACE

BY YVETTE LaPIERRE

AMERICAN CRIME STORIES

Essential Library

An Imprint of Abdo Publishing | abdobooks.com

ABDOBOOKS.COM

Published by Abdo Publishing, a division of ABDO, PO Box 398166, Minneapolis, Minnesota 55439.

Printed in the United States of America, North Mankato, Minnesota.
102023
012024

THIS BOOK CONTAINS RECYCLED MATERIALS

Cover Photo: Leonardo Cendamo/Hulton Archive/Getty Images
Interior Photos: Alan Diaz/AP Images, 5, 49, 89; Gregory Smith/AP Images, 8, 75, 78; Dave M. Benett/Hulton Archive/Getty Images, 11; Richard Ellis/Alamy, 12; E. J. Flynn/AP Images, 15; Hans Deryk/AP Images, 17, 65; Jeffrey Boan/FBI/AP Images, 20; iStockphoto, 23; The Star Tribune/AP Images, 25; John Brueske/iStockphoto, 28; John B. Reilly/Sygma/Getty Images, 31; David Caton/Alamy, 32; Brian K. Diggs/AP Images, 35; Shutterstock Images, 39, 94; FBI/AFP/Getty Images, 42–43; Reed Saxon/AP Images, 45; Bill Cooke/AP Images, 47; Jeffrey Boan/AP Images, 52; Robert Sullivan/AFP/Getty Images, 55, 62; Marta Lavandier/AP Images, 58, 70; Roberto Schmidt/AFP/Getty Images, 69; Peter Bardocz/Shutterstock Images, 73; Angelo Deligio/Mondadori Portfolio/Getty Images, 81; Red Line Editorial, 83; Bishops School/AP Images, 86; Brian Rasic/Hulton Archive/Getty Images, 93; Jordan Strauss/Invision/AP Images, 96

Editor: Laura Stickney
Series Designer: Melissa Martin

Library of Congress Control Number: 2023939442

PUBLISHER'S CATALOGING-IN-PUBLICATION DATA

Names: LaPierre, Yvette, author.
Title: The murder of Gianni Versace / by Yvette LaPierre
Description: Minneapolis, Minnesota: Abdo Publishing, 2024 | Series: American crime stories | Includes online resources and index.
Identifiers: ISBN 9781098292119 (lib. bdg.) | ISBN 9798384910053 (ebook)
Subjects: LCSH: Crime and criminals--Juvenile literature. | Killing (Murder)--Juvenile literature. | United States--Juvenile literature. | Versace, Gianni--Juvenile literature. | Serial murders--Juvenile literature. | Gay men--Crimes against--Juvenile literature. | Serial murder investigation--Juvenile literature.
Classification: DDC 364.97--dc23

CONTENTS

This book discusses accounts of crime, violence, and death that may be disturbing to some readers.

CHAPTER ONE
MURDER IN MIAMI 4

CHAPTER TWO
AMERICA'S MOST WANTED 14

CHAPTER THREE
MURDER SPREE 22

CHAPTER FOUR
GETTING AWAY WITH MURDER 34

CHAPTER FIVE
HIDDEN IN PLAIN SIGHT 46

CHAPTER SIX
MIAMI MANHUNT 54

CHAPTER SEVEN
THE SEARCH ENDS 64

CHAPTER EIGHT
UNKNOWN MOTIVES 74

CHAPTER NINE
CASE CLOSED 88

Timeline 98
Essential Facts 100
Glossary 102
Additional Resources 104
Source Notes 106
Index 110
About the Author 112

CHAPTER ONE

MURDER IN MIAMI

July 15, 1997, began as a typical day for internationally renowned fashion designer Gianni Versace. Versace got up early that morning, as usual. He and his longtime partner, Antonio D'Amico, were enjoying morning coffee in Versace's mansion at 1116 Ocean Drive in the South Beach neighborhood of Miami Beach, Florida. They had arrived in town several days ago.

As he did most mornings in Florida, Versace strolled three blocks south on Ocean Drive to the News Cafe at around 8:30 a.m. He was dressed simply in a T-shirt, black shorts, and sandals. Versace often walked alone on the streets and beaches near his Miami Beach home. He didn't feel the need for bodyguards trailing him or security guards protecting his mansion.

Versace's villa is known for its lavish architecture and interior design. It features a rooftop observatory and a pool made with more than one million mosaic tiles.

PRIVATE

CASA CASUARINA

Versace's mansion, Casa Casuarina, was the only private residence on Ocean Drive in Miami Beach. In 1992, Versace bought an old run-down apartment building that had been built as a grand Mediterranean villa in 1930. He paid $2.9 million for the property. The next year, he paid $3.7 million for the old hotel next door.[2] Versace had the hotel knocked down so he could build a patio and a luxury swimming pool. He spent millions of dollars to turn the apartment building into a lavish Mediterranean-style mansion. Versace had several homes around the world, but he enjoyed coming to Casa Casuarina to relax and take a break from his busy life.

At the News Cafe, Versace spent about $15.00 on five magazines: *Business Week*, *Entertainment Weekly*, *People*, the *New Yorker*, and *Vogue*.[1] Then he started walking back toward home at about 8:40 a.m. Versace smiled at a neighbor, Mersiha Colakovic, as he passed her and reached the gate to his villa a few minutes later. Across the street was a man wearing shorts and a tank top over a baggy gray T-shirt. He had a black baseball cap pulled down low over his eyes, along with a black backpack slung over his right shoulder.

A Shooting in Broad Daylight

Versace walked up the four front steps of his villa and reached the mansion's ornate wrought iron gates. Just as Versace was fitting the key into the gate lock, the man from across the street quickly approached him. He came up from behind Versace and pulled out a handgun.

Gianni Versace grew up in a modest home in Italy. His mother ran a dressmaking business, and his father was a coal merchant.

Holding the gun out straight, the man shot Versace once in the neck behind his left ear and cheek. Versace may have turned to face his attacker. The man shot a second time, hitting Versace on the right side of his face, next to his nose. Versace immediately slumped to the steps, unconscious. His neighbor Colakovic witnessed the shooting from less than 30 feet (9 m) away.[3]

Inside the villa, D'Amico jumped at the sound of the gunfire. The house had stained glass windows, so he was not able to see what had happened outside. He rushed outside to the front gates and found Versace lying in a pool of blood. "I saw Gianni lying on the steps, with blood around him," D'Amico said. "At that point, everything went dark. I was pulled away, I didn't see any more."[4] The couple's cook called 911 at 8:44 a.m. Within two minutes, police arrived on bikes at the scene of the crime.

The Shooter Escapes

In the meantime, the shooter had put the gun in his backpack and calmly started walking away down Ocean Drive. Another neighbor rushed over to see what had happened.

Officers from the Miami Beach Police Department put yellow crime scene tape around the villa's front steps to block off the area.

Colakovic pointed toward the shooter. The neighbor started following the man at a distance. The shooter turned left onto Twelfth Street and cut left into an alley. Then he turned right into another alley and was briefly caught on a hotel's security camera. He headed toward the Thirteenth Street city parking garage. At some point, he turned and pointed his gun at the neighbor, but he didn't fire. The neighbor then gave up the chase.

Other witnesses reported seeing the shooter enter the parking garage a few blocks away from Versace's mansion. He slipped past police officers who were already at the garage responding to a minor car accident. Witnesses saw the shooter get into a red truck, quickly change clothes, and flee from the parking garage on foot.

Family, Friends, and Fans Mourn

Miami Beach Police officer Calvin Lincoln was one of the first officers to arrive on the scene. He checked Versace's pulse and breathing but found no signs of life. Paramedics kept Versace's heart beating as he was rushed to the Jackson Memorial Hospital's Ryder Trauma Center in Miami, just seven miles (11.3 km) away.[5] Shortly after his arrival, doctors pronounced Versace dead. He was 50 years old.

As the news of Versace's death spread, family, friends, and fans in Miami and around the world expressed their grief. Versace's famous friends and clients, such as Princess Diana, Elton John, and Madonna, commented on their shock and dismay. So did one of Versace's fashion design competitors, Giorgio Armani. He said, "Gianni Versace, together with a handful of names, symbolizes the success of Italian fashion all over the world. My reaction is one of revolt against such an unnatural and violent death and one of profound grief."[6]

The bloodstained steps of Versace's villa drew hundreds of onlookers. The designer's beloved retreat was now under siege. Dozens of reporters and photographers lined the street.

Versace launched his clothing label in 1978. He quickly became one of the world's most successful designers.

Television news helicopters circled overhead. Local police and Federal Bureau of Investigation (FBI) agents swarmed the grounds. Later in the afternoon, a county worker scrubbed Versace's blood off the coral steps. A makeshift memorial appeared on the clean steps as people piled flowers and cards there. They lit candles in memory of the man gunned down in front of his house in broad daylight.

Motives

Miami Beach Police detective Paul Scrimshaw was put in charge of the murder investigation. He immediately began to consider possible motives for the crime. One theory was that Versace, who had been born in Italy, was the victim of the Mafia. This is a society of organized crime groups that formed in Italy in the

MAFIA HIT?

When police first arrived on the murder scene, they thought it looked much like a murder for hire. Versace had been shot in the head at close range. Near his body was a mourning dove that had been recently killed. Police knew that a dead bird was a traditional Mafia symbol. As a result, the FBI was called to help investigate the murder. Agents looked for clues to help determine if Versace's murder was a random killing or a Mafia hit.

late 1800s and later became established in the United States. Another motive could have been robbery, since Versace was a wealthy man.

Versace was also openly gay. At the time, some people held stereotypes about members of the LGBTQ+ community that associated them with the AIDS epidemic. These stereotypes contributed to speculation among some police officers that Versace could have given the killer HIV, the virus that causes

Versace had close friendships with many celebrities, including supermodels Naomi Campbell, *left*, and Carla Bruni, *right*, who frequently appeared in his fashion shows. Both models attended Versace's funeral.

After police removed the crime scene tape around the villa steps, many mourners left bouquets, candles, gifts, and handwritten notes in honor of Versace. Some people also left flowers outside Versace stores.

AIDS, and been killed in revenge. However, it was not known whether Versace was even infected with this virus.

It was also possible that the killing had been a completely random act of violence. Versace and other people in his house had regular routines. Anyone stalking Versace would know what times he usually left the house and returned home. People who knew Versace also said that he disliked security. According to one source, Versace "didn't like having someone standing over him. He thought security isolated him from the people."[7] Versace also didn't like to have the villa's security cameras turned on. This meant that police were not able to review any video footage from the cameras for clues. In the immediate aftermath of the murder, the police had no idea who had killed Versace—or why.

CHAPTER TWO

AMERICA'S MOST WANTED

Versace's murder sent shock waves throughout the South Beach community and the local police department. Murders were uncommon in the area. And Versace's murder had been very public. In broad daylight and in the presence of witnesses, the killer had walked right up to Versace, shot him twice, and then calmly walked away. Because of the bold nature of the crime, police immediately thought they might be dealing with a trained, professional assassin.

The police department quickly called in the FBI. Within hours of the killing, authorities had a prime suspect in the murder of Versace. The suspect wasn't a professional killer, but he was no stranger to the FBI and other law enforcement agencies.

After authorities named Cunanan as the prime suspect in Versace's murder, many people put up wanted posters with pictures of Cunanan on them.

WANTED
City of West Hollywood
California 1984
CUNANAN, ANDREW PHILLIP
SUSPECT: Andrew Phillip Cunanan
Male, White, D.O.B. 08-31-69
Brown Hair, Brown Eyes, 5'9", 160 lbs.
SUSPECT IS CONSIDERED ARMED AND EXTREMELY DANGEROUS.
IF SEEN, DO NOT ATTEMPT TO APPREHEND.
IMMEDIATELY CONTACT WEST HOLLYWOOD SHERIFF'S STATION
AT (310) 855-8850, OR CALL 911.
Please Check
All Bags Behin
The Counter
Thank You!

The Red Truck

Police quickly responded to witness reports that Versace's killer had run toward the Thirteenth Street parking garage. Some police were already on the scene for the car accident. Other officers arrived by 8:56 a.m. Soon there were officers covering the garage, its exits, and the nearby alley. At first, there was some confusion about what the suspect looked like. But some witnesses described the shooter as a white man with brown hair in his mid-20s. The police searched the area for a man matching this description, but they didn't find anybody.

On the third level of the parking garage, police officers found a pile of clothes next to a red truck. The clothes matched what witnesses said the killer was wearing: a black tank top, a gray T-shirt, and shorts. The T-shirt appeared to be damp with perspiration, indicating that it had been worn very recently. Inside the truck, on the floor of the driver's side, the officers

VERSACE'S FUNERAL

Versace's funeral was held on Tuesday, July 22, one week after his murder. About 2,000 mourners attended the funeral, which was held at the magnificent Roman Catholic cathedral in Milan, Italy.[1] Many of Versace's famous friends and clients attended, including Naomi Campbell, Princess Diana, Elton John, and Sting. Some of Versace's fellow fashion designers also attended. Versace's sister, Donatella Versace, arranged the funeral. She said, "Gianni was killed like a stray dog. I want him to have a funeral fit for a prince."[2]

could see a black backpack. Miami Beach Police chief Richard Barreto assumed the killer had been in a state of panic when he saw the police. "I'm sure he saw police everywhere and fled for his life," Barreto said.[3]

The police ran a check on the truck's South Carolina license plate, but the plate didn't match any in their database or provide any clues about the truck's owner. Officers decided to check the truck's Vehicle Identification Number (VIN). Every vehicle is given a unique VIN when it is manufactured. The VIN can be used to track vehicle registrations, insurance coverage, and warranties, among other information. Police can use a vehicle's VIN to see if it has been stolen or involved in a crime.

Spectators watched as police towed the red Chevrolet pickup truck away from the Thirteenth Street parking garage.

Collecting Evidence

Police searched inside the red truck and collected several pieces of incriminating evidence. The most notable discovery was a passport issued to Andrew Phillip Cunanan. They also discovered a check with Cunanan's name printed on it. A ticket found inside the truck showed that it had been parked in the garage just blocks away from Versace's home since June 10, almost five weeks ago.

Meanwhile, FBI agents worked with investigators from the Florida Department of Law Enforcement to process the murder scene back at Versace's villa. They recovered two .40 caliber brass bullet casings from the scene.[4] One casing was found on the villa's front step, while the other was found in the street.

According to his family, Cunanan had read a whole set of encyclopedias by age ten and memorized long passages from them.

Soon police received the results of the VIN search. The red truck matched a vehicle that had been stolen in New Jersey on May 9. The truck was registered to a man named William Reese, who had been found shot to death on the same day his truck was stolen. The main suspect in Reese's murder and in the theft of the truck was Andrew Cunanan. Detective Scrimshaw knew immediately that Cunanan must be linked to Versace's murder in some way.

Prime Suspect

Within two hours of the murder, the authorities focused on Cunanan. He was wanted in connection with four murders across the country. He was the subject of a nationwide manhunt. He had even been featured on the television program *America's Most Wanted*. Now it appeared that Cunanan had been living in Miami Beach for more than a month and had struck again.

But the police did not release Cunanan's name to the media and the public right away. The Florida State Attorney's Office wanted the police to proceed cautiously with the investigation. If Cunanan came to trial for Versace's murder, they didn't want the case compromised for any reason, such as releasing information to the media and public too soon. Laws govern what information law enforcement agencies can release during an active investigation. Withholding details allows the investigation to continue unhindered and protects the privacy

ANDREW CUNANAN

Andrew Cunanan was born in 1969 and was the youngest of four children raised in a middle-class family in San Diego, California. As a child, Cunanan loved to read and had a high IQ when he was tested in elementary school. He attended a prestigious private high school in San Diego, where most of his classmates were much wealthier than he was. He was a popular student with lots of friends. Cunanan began college after high school, but he soon dropped out.

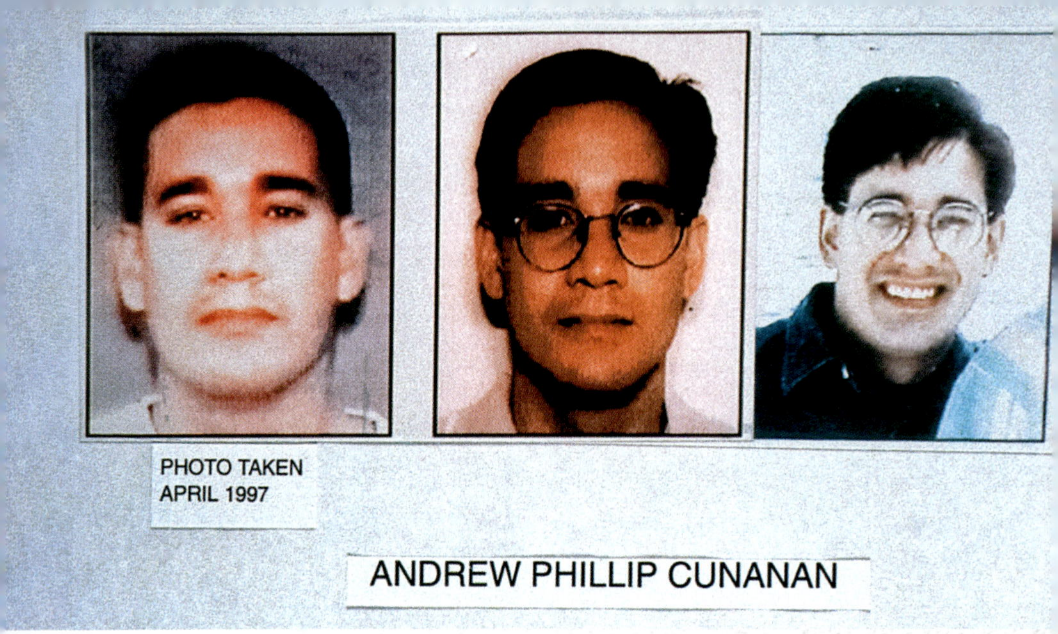

Investigators shared several pictures of Cunanan with the public. Based on reports from Cunanan's acquaintances, police described him as having eyeglasses, a loud laugh, and expensive tastes.

of victims and witnesses. If the police violate any rules, criminal charges may be dropped in court.

Armed and Dangerous

The Miami Beach Police issued two press releases announcing Versace's death and the ongoing investigation without naming any suspects. Finally, at 8:30 p.m., the Miami Beach Police held a third press conference where they named Cunanan as the main suspect in the murder of Versace. The police described the suspect as a 27-year-old white male who was about 5 feet 9 or 10 inches (1.75 m–1.78 m) tall with brown hair and brown eyes. They said Cunanan was known to be well-dressed, well-educated, and articulate. According to friends, family, and acquaintances interviewed by the FBI, Cunanan was very charming and wanted to live a life of wealth and luxury. He appeared to have funded his lifestyle by having relationships with wealthy older men. The police reported that according to acquaintances, Cunanan may have been working as a prostitute before beginning a killing spree in Minneapolis, Minnesota, the previous April.

A COMMUNITY ON ALERT

The police warned the public that Cunanan was extremely dangerous and likely to kill again, but they couldn't predict when, where, or whom he might strike next. They weren't sure if Cunanan was still in the Miami Beach area or if he had moved on. In addition, the murders he'd committed so far didn't follow a set pattern. Cunanan might murder someone he knew, but he might also murder someone just so he could steal their car. One community, however, was especially concerned. Cunanan was openly gay, as were Versace and some of Cunanan's other victims. The FBI warned the LGBTQ+ community to be on the lookout for Cunanan.

During the news conference, Chief Barreto told the press that Cunanan "should be considered armed and dangerous. He is already wanted for four murders, and that should be of concern to the community."[5] With Cunanan on the loose, everyone was at risk. But by the time the public was warned, Cunanan had had all day to plan his next move.

Although he dropped out of college, Cunanan was an intelligent man. He was well-read and could speak two languages.

CHAPTER THREE

MURDER SPREE

On April 24, 1997, about three months before the Versace killing, Andrew Cunanan invited his friends to a restaurant in San Diego. He was throwing himself a farewell party, even though he didn't have enough money to pay for the gathering. He had decided to move from his hometown, San Diego, to San Francisco, California.

Cunanan told his friends that before moving, he was flying to Minneapolis to visit two old friends. He planned to visit Jeffrey Trail and David Madson. Trail was 28 years old and had dark hair. He was a graduate of the US Naval Academy. He and Cunanan had been good friends when Trail lived in the San Diego area, but Trail had moved to Minneapolis for a new job. Madson was a 33-year-old architect with blond hair. According to interviews with Cunanan's friends in California, Madson and Cunanan had dated and broken up the previous spring. The breakup had left Cunanan heartbroken.

David Madson lived in the Harmony Lofts building in the Warehouse District of Minneapolis, Minnesota. Also called the North Loop neighborhood, this area is known for its bars, historic buildings, and nightclubs.

the LOOP
BAR RESTAURANT
FOR LEASE

Minneapolis Murders

Cunanan packed just one small black duffel bag for his trip to Minneapolis and boarded a flight on Saturday, April 25. He arrived at about 5:30 p.m., and Madson picked him up at the airport. That evening, Cunanan and Madson went out to dinner and then went dancing. According to some witnesses later interviewed by police, Cunanan may have left the dance club before Madson and gone to see Trail that night. Trail lived in an apartment in nearby Bloomington, Minnesota.

Cunanan was staying at Madson's apartment that weekend. On Sunday, April 27, Cunanan left a message on Trail's telephone answering machine, inviting Trail to meet for coffee that evening. Trail had plans with friends later that night, but he told his roommate he was going to see Cunanan before joining his friends. He left to meet up with Cunanan at 9:00 p.m.

But Trail didn't show up to meet his friends that night, and he didn't go back home to his apartment. Neither Trail

LIFE UNRAVELING

When Cunanan left for his trip to Minnesota in April 1997, he had no criminal record. He was described by friends and acquaintances as charming, stylish, and popular. His lavish lifestyle was funded mostly by wealthy friends and boyfriends. But friends reported that Cunanan changed in the spring of 1997. His last wealthy boyfriend had left him, and he had no visible source of income. He also looked disheveled at times.

nor Madson were at work on Monday morning. Friends and coworkers tried to contact both men but had no luck.

Cunanan purchased a one-way plane ticket to Minneapolis, suggesting he did not plan to return to California.

On Tuesday, April 29, Madson failed to show up to work for a second day. Two of his coworkers went to his home to check on him. They knocked on the door. No one answered, but

According to friends and family, Trail was a kind, fun-loving young man. Cunanan reportedly said that Trail was like a brother to him.

they could hear Madson's dog inside pawing and scratching at the door. Worried that something was wrong, the two women called the police. When the police arrived, they warned Madson's coworkers that if they forced the door open and the dog became aggressive, they would have to kill it. The women didn't want to risk that, so they let the police leave and called the building's caretaker instead. She arrived at about 4:00 p.m. and unlocked the door to Madson's apartment. Right away, the women saw bloody footprints on the hardwood floor. Then they spotted a body rolled up in an Oriental rug. They called the police again.

About 20 minutes later, Minneapolis police officers returned to Madson's apartment and notified the homicide department that a body had been found. Sergeant Bob Tichich called in forensic technicians to photograph the body and process the apartment while he and the officers made a quick examination of the scene. Tichich assumed that the body must be Madson, who had been missing from work for two days.

In addition to the bloody footprints, blood was splattered on the front door. Tichich determined that the victim had been attacked at the front door, rolled up in the rug, and then dragged about 10 feet (3 m) into the living room.[1] The police also noted that while Madson's dog was in the apartment, there were no traces of urine or feces. Clearly, the dog had not been trapped in the apartment for two days.

That same day, police officers in Bloomington, Minnesota, filed a missing person report for Trail, who had been missing since Sunday night. The next day, the body found in Madson's apartment was prepared for autopsy. It was lifted from the bloody rug for the first time, and the medical examiner could see that the victim's hair was dark, not blond like Madson's. In the back pocket of the victim's jeans, the examiner found a black nylon wallet. It contained some money and Trail's ID.

A careful examination of the body revealed that the victim had been hit on the face, head, and upper torso a total of 27 times with a hammer that had been found in the apartment.[2] The first blow to his head landed with great force. Trail had been hit several times on his left wrist and hand too. He had clearly raised his arms to protect himself from the blows before falling to the ground and being bludgeoned to death.

The body was positively identified as Trail, and Madson went from being the assumed victim to being the

PROCESSING A MURDER SCENE

Crime scene investigators and technicians photograph, collect, and preserve physical evidence present at a crime scene. The first step is an initial walk through the scene to identify potential evidence, such as strands of hair, blood splatters, or bullet casings. The experts take photographs and jot down notes. Next, they thoroughly document the scene with cameras and dust it for fingerprints. Investigators carefully collect and log all pieces of physical evidence. This evidence may be presented in court as part of a criminal case.

murder suspect. That night, police issued an alert for authorities to be on the lookout for Madson in a red Jeep Grand Cherokee. He was wanted in connection with the murder of Trail.

Over the next few days, the search for Madson yielded no results. Based on interviews with Madson's friends, the police thought he might be accompanied by a friend, Andrew Cunanan. On Saturday morning, May 3, two fishermen discovered a body in tall grass behind an abandoned farmhouse on the edge of East Rush Lake. This was about an hour away from Minneapolis. The victim was lying on his back and was fully clothed in jeans and a plaid shirt. The men called 911, and officers from the local Chisago County Sheriff's Office came to the scene. The victim had been shot three times—in the right eye, the right cheek, and the back between

Madson's body was found in a remote spot by East Rush Lake, near Rush City, Minnesota. Investigators were puzzled by this location.

the shoulder blades. Marks on the ground suggested that the victim had then been dragged 20 feet (6 m) from the spot where he was shot.[3]

No identification was found with the victim, but his physical characteristics matched those of Madson, who was slender and blond. Car keys and a keyless-entry device for a Jeep Grand Cherokee were found near the body. The vehicle was gone, and police had a new murder suspect—Andrew Cunanan.

ACCOMPLICE?

Even after Madson's body was discovered, authorities wondered if Madson had been involved in Trail's murder. An autopsy on Madson's body placed the probable time and date of his death as late Friday, May 2. That would indicate that Cunanan and Madson had been together for five days after Trail's murder on April 27. Some witnesses reported seeing the two men walking a dog together. That could mean both men were responsible for Trail's death. Another possibility was that only one of the men was the murderer and the other was an accomplice.

Murder in Chicago

An autopsy confirmed that the body found at East Rush Lake was Madson. On the morning of May 4, police issued a nationwide criminal advisory for Cunanan. The advisory said that Cunanan might be going by the name DeSilva, an alias that friends said Cunanan often used. It also said he might be driving a red Jeep Grand Cherokee with a Minnesota license plate. The advisory stated that Cunanan was wanted in connection with two murders in Minnesota and that he should be considered armed and dangerous.

That same day, Marilyn Miglin returned to her home in Chicago, Illinois, after a short trip. She had taken a taxi because her husband, Lee Miglin, had failed to pick her up from the airport. The Miglins had been married for 37 years and had two grown children. Lee was a wealthy real estate developer, and Marilyn had a successful beauty business.

When Marilyn entered the house, she couldn't find her husband. But she discovered disturbing evidence that someone had been there. The house was a mess. Frightened, Marilyn called the police and left to ask a neighbor to help her look around the house. They found Lee's clothes and shoes strewn about. There were dirty dishes all over the normally neat kitchen. In an upstairs bathroom, they saw a gun in the sink among black whiskers. But Lee had white hair.

Criminal advisories are warnings of crimes that represent an ongoing threat to the safety of others.

When Chicago police officers arrived to search the home, the neighbor let an officer into the Miglins' garage. There, they found Lee's body underneath a car. His hands and feet had been bound with a tightly knotted orange extension cord, and his mouth had been gagged with a gardening glove. Lee's face

Lee Miglin was a wealthy, widely respected man known for his real estate development work. He and his wife lived in a brownstone mansion in Chicago's Gold Coast neighborhood.

had been wrapped with masking tape like a mummy, with only holes for his nostrils. He had been stabbed many times in the chest, and his throat had been slashed almost all the way through.

Police examined the couple's garage and home and dusted for fingerprints. Fingerprints found on the property, however, did not provide any clues to the identity of Miglin's killer. There were also no broken windows, doors, or locks to indicate that entry to the home had been forced. This meant that either the suspect had found the home unlocked or Miglin had let him in. The only thing that appeared to be missing from the house was Miglin's car, a dark green Lexus sedan, along with some clothes and money. But the crime did not appear to be a typical robbery. Based on the evidence, it seemed like the

Finn's Point National Cemetery is home to historic graves and monuments dating back to the American Civil War (1861–1865). William Reese was the only caretaker who worked at the cemetery.

murderer had been in no hurry to leave the scene of the crime. Dirty sheets, wet towels, and whiskers in the sink suggested that after killing Miglin, the murderer had slept in a bed, taken a bath, and even shaved. The Chicago police had no suspect in the crime.

Three days later, on May 7, a police officer noticed a red Jeep Grand Cherokee parked around the corner from Miglin's house. Three parking tickets were found on the car.[4] The officer ran a check on the car's license plates and discovered that it belonged to David Madson, the victim of a murder by wanted suspect Andrew Cunanan. This discovery was shared with other police departments involved in the case. The authorities were now looking for Cunanan in a stolen Lexus with Illinois license plates.

New Jersey Cemetery

On Friday, May 9, 45-year-old William Reese did not come home from work as he did every day. Reese was the caretaker at the remote Finn's Point National Cemetery near Pennsville, New Jersey. Reese's wife decided to drive to the cemetery to look for him. She drove down a long, narrow dirt road through deep woods to get to the historic Civil War site. She expected to see her husband's red 1995 Chevrolet truck. Instead, she saw only an unfamiliar dark green Lexus parked at the cemetery. She immediately called the police and waited until they arrived.

Local police officers responded and found Reese lying in a pool of blood on the concrete floor of the cemetery office's basement. He had been shot in the back of the head. Pennsville police ran a check on the Lexus license plate. They quickly learned that the car belonged to Miglin. Cunanan had struck again for the fourth time in two weeks, this time at an isolated spot in New Jersey.

The authorities updated the criminal advisory for Cunanan. He was now traveling in the New Jersey vicinity in Reese's vehicle. Cunanan was killing fast and on the move again. The urgent search for the fugitive continued.

CHAPTER FOUR

GETTING AWAY WITH MURDER

For almost a week after Trail's body was found on April 29, Minneapolis police officers had focused their efforts on locating Madson, who was their main suspect in the murder. This had allowed Cunanan to move freely. But after Madson's body was discovered, authorities shifted the focus of their search to Cunanan. The police were now working under the assumption that Cunanan was killing men he knew.

One possible motive that investigators considered was a love triangle between Cunanan, Trail, and Madson. A love triangle could have led to jealousy and anger. One acquaintance reported that Cunanan was extremely angry because he had learned he had HIV. This made some people wonder if Cunanan was killing men who could have given him the virus in order to get revenge.

William Esposito was deputy director of the FBI during the search for Cunanan. He spoke about the case at news conferences.

NO FINGERPRINTS

Forensic technicians dusted for fingerprints at Trail's apartment, the scenes of the four murders, and the vehicles Cunanan drove. Authorities check prints found at a crime scene against prints in police and FBI fingerprint databases. These databases contain prints that have been collected at other crime scenes. Because Cunanan didn't have a criminal record, fingerprints collected at the crime scenes resulted in no matches. The only fingerprint available for Cunanan was his right thumbprint, which had been taken when he got his California driver's license.

Miglin's murder changed the trajectory of the investigation. Now Cunanan was suspected of killing a wealthy man in Chicago who, as far as anyone knew, was heterosexual and unknown to Cunanan. The search for the killer was becoming a high-profile case, involving police departments in Minneapolis, Chicago, and Chisago County, Minnesota.

The Chisago County Attorney's Office determined that it had enough evidence to request a warrant for Cunanan's arrest. As a result of the arrest warrant, the FBI became involved in the case on May 7. The investigation expanded into a national manhunt. As the number of victims grew, the FBI and police began piecing together the evidence. And there was plenty of it.

Gathering Evidence

The first pieces of evidence were collected at Madson's apartment, where Trail's body was found. Police technicians photographed the body, dusted for fingerprints, and processed the apartment, while police made a quick walk-through of the entire apartment to collect evidence. From the blood splatter pattern, it was clear that Trail had been savagely beaten by the front door. Then he had been rolled up in a carpet that was normally kept by the front door and dragged past the dining room into the living room. Police found cloth and paper towels that had been used in an attempt to clean up all the blood. Despite that, they also found two sets of bloody footprints—one set with shoes, and one set of bare feet.[1]

Under the table, police discovered a plastic drawstring bag that contained towels, a Banana Republic T-shirt, and a hammer, all covered in blood. Trail's watch and US Navy ring were also in the bag. Cunanan had clearly not made any attempt to hide or dispose of the murder weapon. In a bedroom, police found a black duffel bag that contained, among other items, an empty gun holster and a box of .40 caliber Remington Golden Saber bullets. Ten bullets were missing from the box.[2]

On May 3, police officers processed the site on East Rush Lake where Madson's body had been found. Police found one .40 caliber Golden Saber bullet casing near tire marks in the grass.[3]

Forensic experts use bloodstain pattern analysis to help figure out the story of a crime scene. The size and shape of bloodstains can provide important clues about the crime.

A couple of days later, they found another casing using a metal detector. Police searched the lake for the murder weapon but did not recover it.

Madson's Jeep Grand Cherokee, which had been found around the corner from Miglin's murder site, yielded more evidence. First, the vehicle was dusted for fingerprints and photographed on-site. Then it was towed to a police lot for a thorough search. Most of the items found in the Jeep belonged to Madson, except for a map of Chicago that included Miglin's neighborhood. The most interesting discovery was a ticket stub for a parking garage in Chicago. The ticket was marked 6:08 a.m. on April 30, about 12 hours after Trail's body was found and two days before experts estimated that Madson was shot in Minnesota.[4]

Evidence recovered at the scene of Reese's murder further linked all four victims to Cunanan. In the cemetery basement, police found a .40 caliber bullet casing. It was the same type found at both Madson's murder scene and in the black bag at his apartment. Miglin's Lexus, which had been left at the cemetery, was a treasure trove of evidence. The glove box contained Miglin's wallet

The ticket stub found in Madson's Jeep Grand Cherokee threw into doubt the estimated date of May 2 for Madson's murder. It also raised questions about the number of days Madson spent with Cunanan after Trail's murder.

Investigators collected several .40 caliber bullet casings, along with bullet fragments, at each of the crime scenes. This evidence helped them link the murders together.

and credit cards as well as a blank check from Lee and Marilyn Miglin's bank account. In the driver's side door pocket were two pictures of men who were identified as Cunanan's friends.

A plastic bag inside the trunk held bloodied suede gloves, paper towels, and a screwdriver, which police believed was the weapon used to stab Miglin. The bag also contained a white gardening glove that matched the one used to gag Miglin as well as a single black suede shoe that matched the one found on Miglin's body. Cunanan had the time and opportunity to dispose of all this incriminating evidence, yet he chose to leave it behind where he knew police would find it. One FBI agent involved in the case said, "I wouldn't call the case a mystery, because he leaves behind voluminous amounts of evidence."[5]

Missed Evidence

Some of the evidence left behind was initially missed by police investigators. For example, on May 5, police asked a friend of Madson's to come in and identify the black bag found in Madson's apartment. They wanted to make sure the bag belonged to Madson. This was the bag that contained the empty gun holster and the .40 caliber bullets. Police had found it on April 29, the day they found Trail's body in the apartment and searched the home.

They assumed the bag was Madson's, since he was their chief murder suspect at the time. But Madson's friend pointed out an identification tag on the bag's handle. When opened, it revealed the name of the bag's owner: Andrew DeSilva, an alias often used by Cunanan. "Oh, wow," the friend recalled Minneapolis

TRACKING THE LEXUS

Cunanan was almost caught on May 8, just before the Reese murder. Miglin's Lexus had a cellular car phone that immediately activated when the car started. FBI agents were able to track the car with information transmitted from cell phone towers. They alerted Philadelphia police that the car had been tracked into their area. This meant that for the first time, the authorities knew where Cunanan was. Unfortunately, news leaked that the Lexus was being followed. The next time the FBI traced the car, it was near Pennsville, New Jersey. When the car was found at the site of Reese's murder, police discovered that the phone had been tampered with. Police believed Cunanan had heard the leaked news and tried to disable the phone. When he failed to do so, he ditched the Lexus.

Police sergeant Tichich saying. "I'm very embarrassed."[6] If police had checked the bag's tag earlier, suspicion may have shifted from Madson to Cunanan sooner.

Because Trail's body had been found in Madson's apartment, the police had never done a thorough search of Trail's apartment. On May 9, the day that Cunanan killed Reese in New Jersey, friends and family were at Trail's apartment to pack up his belongings. While going through Trail's things in a closet, they found a gun case, metal ammunition box, three gun holsters, and an empty magazine for holding a gun's bullets. They also learned that Trail had purchased a .40 caliber Taurus semiautomatic handgun several years earlier, though the gun itself wasn't in his apartment.

By this time, police had found .40 caliber casings at two murder scenes. They believed the bullets had been fired by the same weapon. Now, police suspected that the gun and ammunition used in the murders belonged to Trail, Cunanan's friend and first victim. According to Minneapolis Police sergeant Steve Wagner, "We didn't have the gun, but we knew it was .40 caliber, and it's an unusual gun."[7]

More critical pieces of evidence went unnoticed until late June, when Madson's friends and family were at his apartment gathering his belongings. In the bathroom, they found two toiletry bags that police had missed. One belonged to Madson and one to Cunanan. This was physical evidence that once

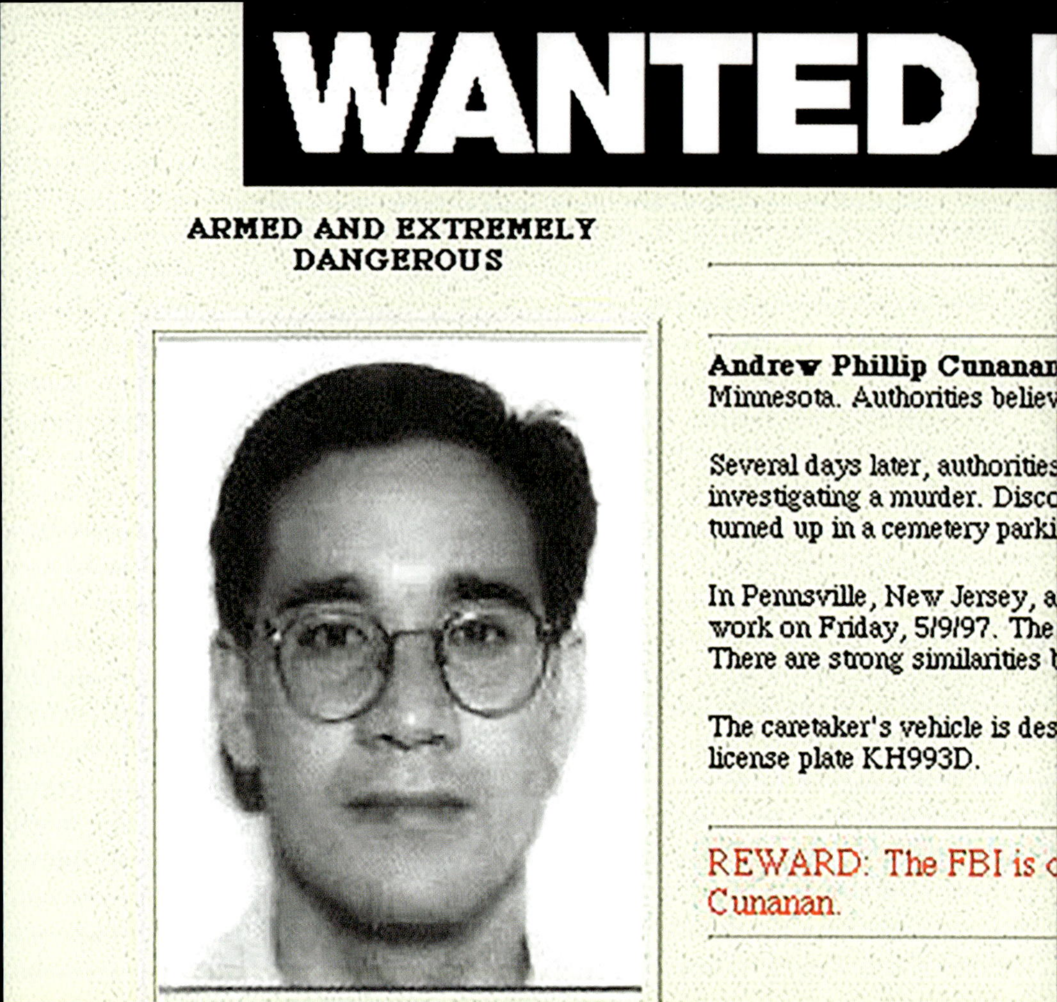
WANTED

ARMED AND EXTREMELY DANGEROUS

Andrew Phillip Cunanan
Minnesota. Authorities
Several days later, authorities
investigating a murder.
turned up in a cemetery
In Pennsville, New Jersey,
work on Friday, 5/9/97. The
There are strong similarities
The caretaker's vehicle is
license plate KH993D.
REWARD: The FBI is
Cunanan.

Investigators shared information about Cunanan on the FBI's website, describing him as armed and dangerous. They also offered a $10,000 reward for any information that could lead to Cunanan's capture.

again linked the two men together. More importantly, Madson's friends and family discovered a pair of Levi's jeans covered in dried blood. The jeans were a size 36 and likely belonged to Cunanan, since Madson wore a size 32. If the blood-soaked jeans had been discovered earlier, it would likely have thrown suspicion on Cunanan as Trail's murderer. "The pants were overlooked," admitted Sergeant Tichich.[8]

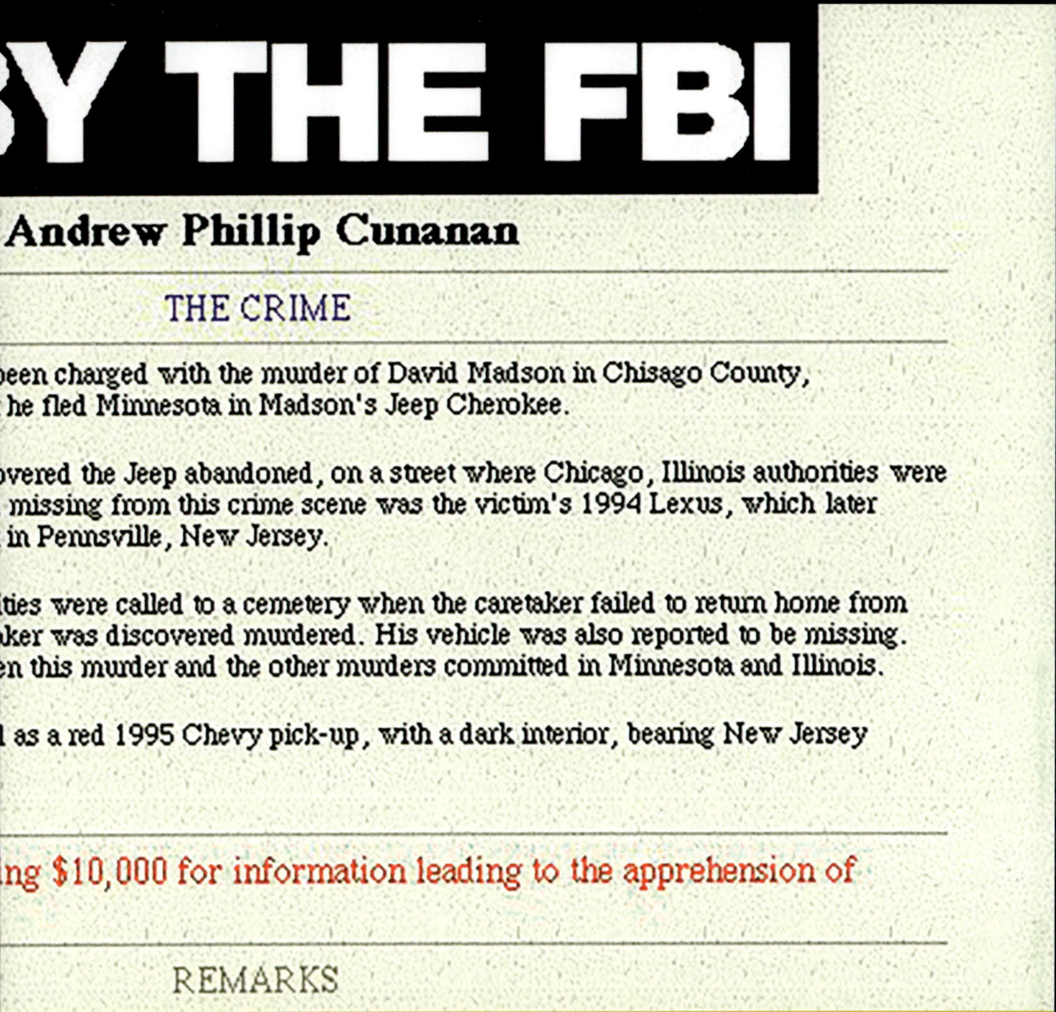
Y THE FBI

Andrew Phillip Cunanan

THE CRIME

een charged with the murder of David Madson in Chisago County,
he fled Minnesota in Madson's Jeep Cherokee.

vered the Jeep abandoned, on a street where Chicago, Illinois authorities were
missing from this crime scene was the victim's 1994 Lexus, which later
in Pennsville, New Jersey.

ties were called to a cemetery when the caretaker failed to return home from
ker was discovered murdered. His vehicle was also reported to be missing.
en this murder and the other murders committed in Minnesota and Illinois.

l as a red 1995 Chevy pick-up, with a dark interior, bearing New Jersey

ng $10,000 for information leading to the apprehension of

REMARKS

National Manhunt Begins

When the FBI became involved in the case, the investigation expanded into a nationwide manhunt. The FBI, in collaboration with several police departments in California, Minnesota, Illinois, and New Jersey, sought information about Cunanan and his movements. The FBI publicized a special telephone tip line and put up pictures of Cunanan on its public website. It distributed thousands of flyers featuring photos of Cunanan and details about him. FBI officers across the country interviewed Cunanan's friends, family, and acquaintances.

The FBI knew that Cunanan was moving quickly across the country. From Minnesota, he drove to Chicago. After killing Miglin and stealing his car, Cunanan apparently drove straight to New York City. At 12:45 a.m. on May 5, he checked into the West Side Club in Chelsea and went to see some movies. The FBI contacted the New York City Anti-Violence Project (AVP), an organization that seeks to make LGBTQ+ communities safer and support people affected by violence. The police sought the group's help in warning its members about Cunanan and the risk he might pose to the community. Then police tracked the Lexus to the Philadelphia area on May 8. Cunanan's next stop was New Jersey.

The intense search for Cunanan attracted the attention of the television show *America's Most*

AMERICA'S MOST WANTED

The original *America's Most Wanted* television program aired from 1988 to 2011. It was a hit series viewed by millions. The first episode aired on February 7, 1988, and the convicted killer featured in the episode was captured four days later as a result of the publicity. A 2005 article by a University of Chicago researcher concluded that a fugitive's appearance on the show made them seven times more likely to be caught.[9] According to the FBI, 17 people on its Ten Most Wanted Fugitives list were captured as a result of tips provided by viewers of the show.[10]

During the search for Cunanan, *America's Most Wanted* was hosted by John Walsh. Walsh would later speak to reporters about his thoughts on the killer.

Wanted, which broadcast its first episode about Cunanan on May 10. The show included photos and actor reenactments of dangerous criminals wanted by the FBI. Each episode ended with a toll-free telephone hotline number that viewers could call if they had any information about the featured criminals.

On May 17, the FBI issued an all-points bulletin (APB) for Cunanan. An APB is an electronic message sent to law enforcement agencies across a wide area to alert them that a suspect is actively being sought in connection with a crime. By that time, Cunanan was living in the Normandy Plaza Hotel in Miami Beach, just blocks away from Versace's mansion.

CHAPTER FIVE

HIDDEN IN PLAIN SIGHT

Police in several states were on the lookout for Cunanan, so authorities thought it would be easy to find him leaving the remote Pennsville area in a bright red truck. But he managed to get out of New Jersey without being seen, and police had no idea where Cunanan might be headed next. The FBI searched for Reese's pickup truck in parking lots at airports, hotels, shopping centers, and bus terminals between Boston and New Jersey. On May 10, authorities received a tip from the public that Cunanan had been seen speeding south on Interstate 95 in a red truck. The caller recognized him from *America's Most Wanted*.

On that same day, Cunanan stopped at a Walmart parking lot in South Carolina just off I-95. He stole a South Carolina license plate from a car and swapped it for the plate on

During his stay at the Normandy Plaza Hotel, Cunanan reportedly ate fast food and bought cheap vodka from a nearby liquor store. He requested to change rooms three times.

歌舞伎
JAPANESE RESTAURANT
SUSHI BAR
HOTEL
HOTEL
NORMANDY PLAZA
DIAL 911
DEDICATED TO COMMUNITY SERVICE
MIAMI BEACH
POLICE
CROWN VICTORIA
124605
225
225

Reese's truck. Cunanan was now heading south in a stolen truck with stolen plates, which the owner never reported as missing. The numerous law enforcement agencies and FBI agents searching for Cunanan had lost track of him.

Normandy Plaza Hotel

Cunanan covered more than 1,000 miles (1,600 km) in two days in Reese's truck.[1] By May 11, he arrived in Miami Beach. He parked the red truck on the street right in front of the Normandy Plaza Hotel. The vehicle would remain there in plain sight for about a month.

At about 8:00 p.m. on May 12, Cunanan checked into the Normandy Plaza Hotel under an alias. He used a French passport for identification. He carried only a black backpack for luggage and wore shorts, a tank top, and flip-flop sandals. He told Miriam Hernandez, the hotel manager, that he was a tourist, and he used cash to pay for a room for one day.

MASTER OF DISGUISE

Cunanan was of average height and weight and had no obvious distinguishing features, such as a large nose or prominent teeth. He seemed to have the ability to transform his appearance simply by adding glasses, changing his hairstyle, or gaining or losing weight. He could look very different from one photo to the next. He could also be difficult to recognize in person based on photos. Cunanan's ability to blend in and change his looks made the manhunt challenging.

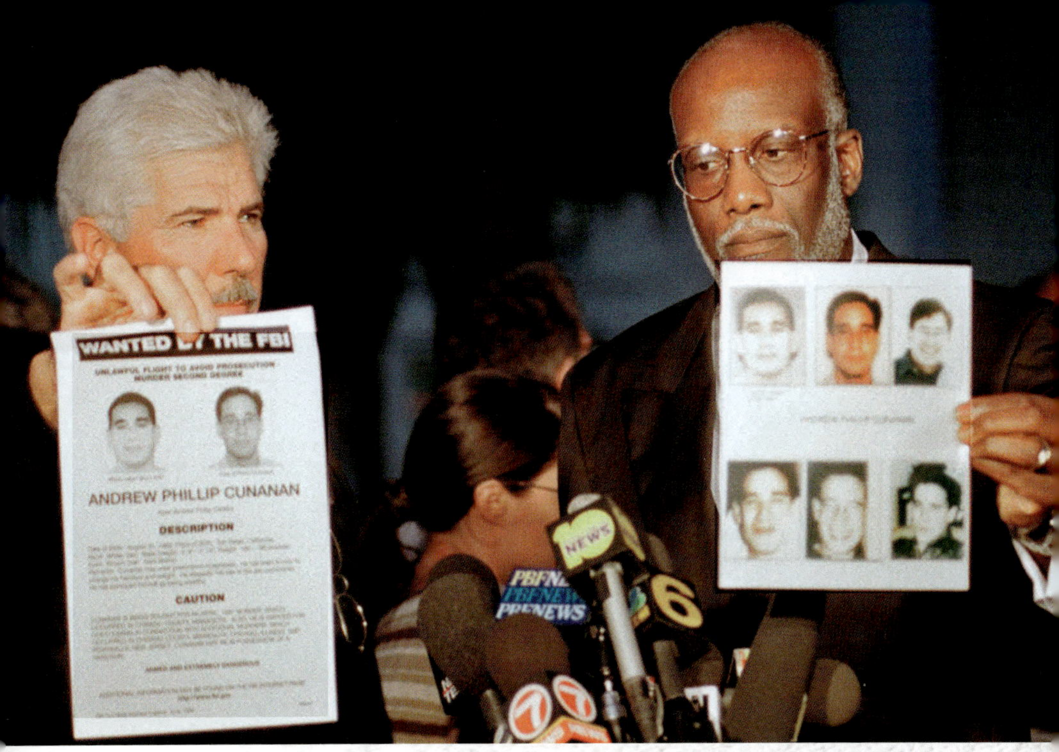

Chief Barreto, *left*, said the search for Cunanan was the biggest case the Miami Beach Police Department had ever worked on. He spoke about the case at press conferences with FBI agent Paul Philip, *right*.

The Normandy was a run-down hotel about four miles (6.4 km) away from Versace's mansion.[2] It had once been a fancy hotel where celebrities such as Marilyn Monroe stayed. Now it was a residential hotel where people could rent cheap rooms for extended stays.

Cunanan stayed in the hotel for about two months, paying by the day.[3] Hotel staff later reported that Cunanan was a quiet and polite guest who caused no problems. He kept his room very tidy and rarely let the maids in to clean. He mostly stayed in his room during the day, reading books and magazines that he bought at a local bookstore. At night, Cunanan would leave by the hotel's back door and go out. He often grabbed a cheap meal, such as a slice of pizza or a tuna melt from a sandwich shop. Some people reported seeing him at local bars and clubs. Little else is known for certain about Cunanan's activities while staying in the hotel.

Despite being the subject of a national manhunt, Cunanan lived openly in Miami Beach for over two months without attracting any notice. The truck he stole from his latest victim, Reese, sat parked on the road for weeks. On June 12, Cunanan moved the truck to the Thirteenth Street parking garage, just blocks from the Versace mansion. He paid $4.00 for one day of parking. But he left the truck in the parking garage for more than a month without anyone checking on it.[4]

Close Calls

Thousands of FBI agents and a dozen law enforcement agencies across the country searched for Cunanan. His face was splashed across flyers and the FBI's website. But even with all the attention, Cunanan was able to roam freely in Miami Beach.

FBI'S MOST WANTED

On June 12, one month after he arrived in Miami Beach, Cunanan made the FBI's Ten Most Wanted Fugitives list. The FBI created this list in 1949 as a way to draw public attention to the country's most dangerous fugitives. Since then, hundreds of criminals have been placed on the list. More than 150 criminals featured on the list have been found as a result of tips received from the public.[5]

The fact that Cunanan committed crimes in multiple states was part of the problem.

The search for Cunanan was based in Minneapolis, where he'd killed his first two victims. All tips and information regarding Cunanan and his whereabouts had to be processed through the investigation office in Minneapolis, and the office was overwhelmed with thousands of tips that needed to be checked. In addition, the investigation required that police departments across the country coordinate and share information, which complicated the investigation. At times, law enforcement agencies disagreed over who should be in charge of crime scenes and evidence.

Andrew Cunanan was the 449th criminal to be named on the FBI's Ten Most Wanted Fugitives list.[6]

But Cunanan had some close calls in Miami Beach. On July 7, Cunanan went to the Cash on the Beach pawn shop, which was located around the corner from the Normandy Plaza Hotel. He pawned a gold coin and was disappointed by the amount of money offered by the pawn shop owner, Vivian Oliva.

But Cunanan accepted the deal and assured Oliva that he would come back to claim the coin. Oliva required a name, address, and identification for paperwork and fingerprints. Cunanan provided a US passport issued to Andrew P. Cunanan as identification. He listed the Normandy Plaza Hotel as his local address, although he gave the incorrect room number. He signed all the papers "Andrew Cunanan."[7]

As required by law, Oliva immediately filed the paperwork with the Miami Beach Police Department and kept the fingerprint card filed at the pawn shop. The paperwork could have alerted police that a man wanted for multiple murders was living in a hotel in Miami Beach. But the forms sat ignored in a pile of paper on a desk.

On July 11, at about 9:00 p.m., an employee at a Miami Subs restaurant near the Normandy Plaza Hotel served a customer. The employee recognized the customer as Cunanan from watching *America's Most Wanted*. As soon as the customer left,

Oliva offered Cunanan $190 for the gold coin. Cunanan agreed to the deal, willingly signing the pawn shop form with his real name. Investigators believed this was a sign that Cunanan was in need of money.

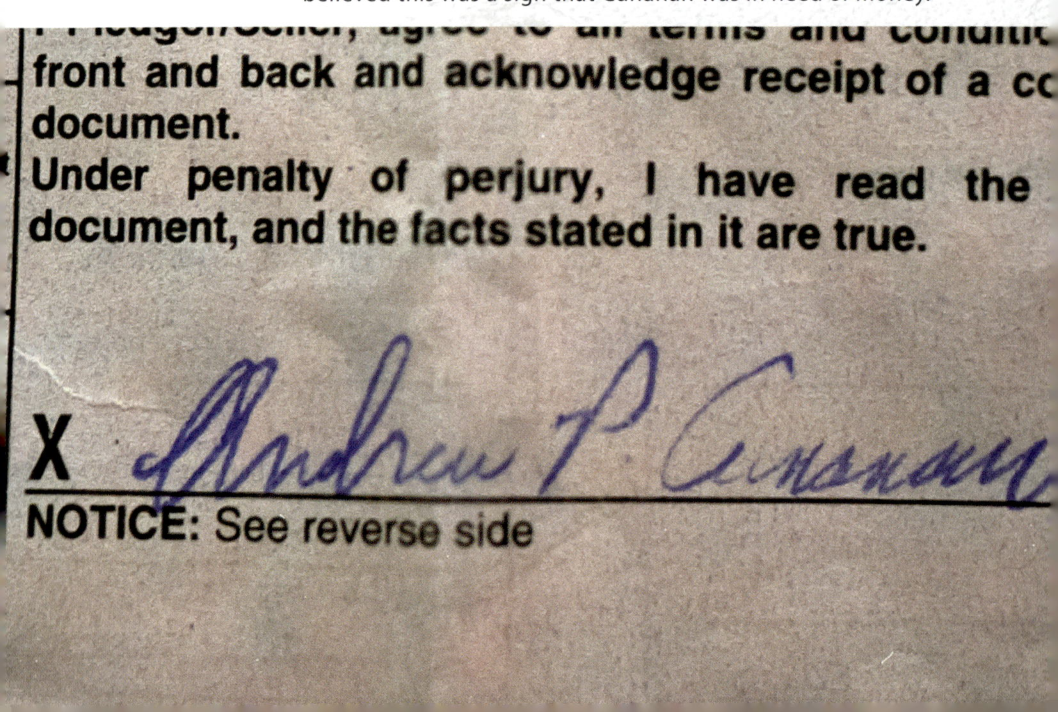
front and back and acknowledge receipt of a co
document.
Under penalty of perjury, I have read the
document, and the facts stated in it are true.

X Andrew P Cunanan

NOTICE: See reverse side

the employee called the Miami Beach Police. Police officers arrived within minutes, but Cunanan was nowhere to be seen.

PAWN SHOP PAPERWORK

Pawn shops gather personal information from customers buying or selling items. This is in order to comply with state and federal laws. Pawn shops file this information with their local police departments. These laws are designed to help police recover stolen items and identify potential thieves. Law enforcement authorities have access to databases of pawned items.

Last Night in the Normandy

Cunanan consistently paid for his hotel room. But on the morning of July 13, two days after he had been recognized by the Miami Subs employee, Cunanan slipped out the back door of the hotel. He did so without paying for his Friday night stay.

When hotel staff checked Cunanan's room, they found the room key on the dresser. Cunanan had also left behind some books and fashion magazines, along with a box for hair clippers. It is possible that Cunanan cut or shaved his hair in an effort to change his appearance. Two days later, Cunanan shot Versace and then quietly disappeared from sight.

On July 10, less than a week before Versace's murder, he and D'Amico arrived in Miami Beach to stay at their villa.

CHAPTER SIX

MIAMI MANHUNT

After Versace's murder on July 15, police and FBI agents fanned out across South Florida in search of Cunanan. His name and photos were shared across the media. According to the FBI, thousands of wanted flyers with Cunanan's name and photo were distributed throughout the Miami area, with a special focus on LGBTQ+ establishments. Undercover detectives enlisted an acquaintance of Cunanan's to accompany them to gay bars in the area, in the hope that Cunanan would approach him. But the plan was unsuccessful.

Many people, especially LGBTQ+ activists, believed that the authorities were not diligent enough about posting flyers and sharing information about Cunanan with the public. Others worried that investigators were overemphasizing stereotypes about gay men, such as homosexual prostitution and contracting AIDS. They feared that prejudice hampered the police response to murders involving gay men. Ronnie Holston,

Investigators distributed 2,000 wanted posters in the Miami area, hoping to raise awareness about Cunanan and encourage Miami residents to be on the lookout for him.

WANTED BY THE FBI
Andrew Phillip Cunanan
Unlawful Flight to Avoid Prosecution - Murder
YOUNG

an acquaintance of Cunanan's, criticized the police response to the case. "The other cops weren't searching so hard, because he killed a bunch of nobody gays," he said.[1]

Owners and patrons of gay bars and nightclubs in South Florida said that they never saw any of the flyers. Many thought that the police and FBI had not taken Cunanan's murder spree seriously until the high-profile murder of Versace. Critics of the police department's performance believed that if the authorities had done a better job, they could have caught Cunanan long before he killed Versace.

On July 16, a sailboat owner in Miami Beach called police to report that a man resembling Cunanan broke into his boat. Police didn't respond to this call or collect evidence for days.

The Miami Beach Police Department was overwhelmed with the media attention on Versace's murder. "We were getting 300 requests a day for interviews and information," said Chief Barreto. "I walked out on my front lawn one day to find it covered with reporters. I've never seen anything like it."[2] Police set up special hotlines for tips about Versace's murder. They asked anyone with information to call the phone lines. Callers submitted thousands of tips, most of them useless. People reported seeing Cunanan in various places around Miami and even around the world.

Pawn Ticket

Not all tips were useless, though. On Wednesday, the day after Versace's murder, Oliva from the Cash on the Beach pawn shop recognized the murder suspect's name as the man who had pawned a gold coin. She called the Miami Beach Police and told them about the form with Cunanan's name and address that she had submitted to them.

Officers came to the shop and collected the coin and fingerprint card as evidence. The police found the form Oliva had submitted on a desk at the police station. It had been left unread since July 10, almost a week before Versace's murder. At that time, the Miami Beach Police Department did not have a computer database for pawn shop forms. All paper forms were filed by hand in a cabinet at the police station.

MURDERED DOCTOR

The hunt for Versace's killer was temporarily complicated by another Miami murder. On July 17, two days after Versace's shooting, a doctor was found strangled in his home in nearby Miami Springs. Witnesses reported seeing a young man who matched Cunanan's description running from the home after a burglar alarm sounded. But evidence found near the scene of the crime led police to arrest another man for the doctor's murder.

The police detective in charge of pawn shop forms had taken a few days off after the form had been submitted and hadn't had time to process it. When the detective returned to

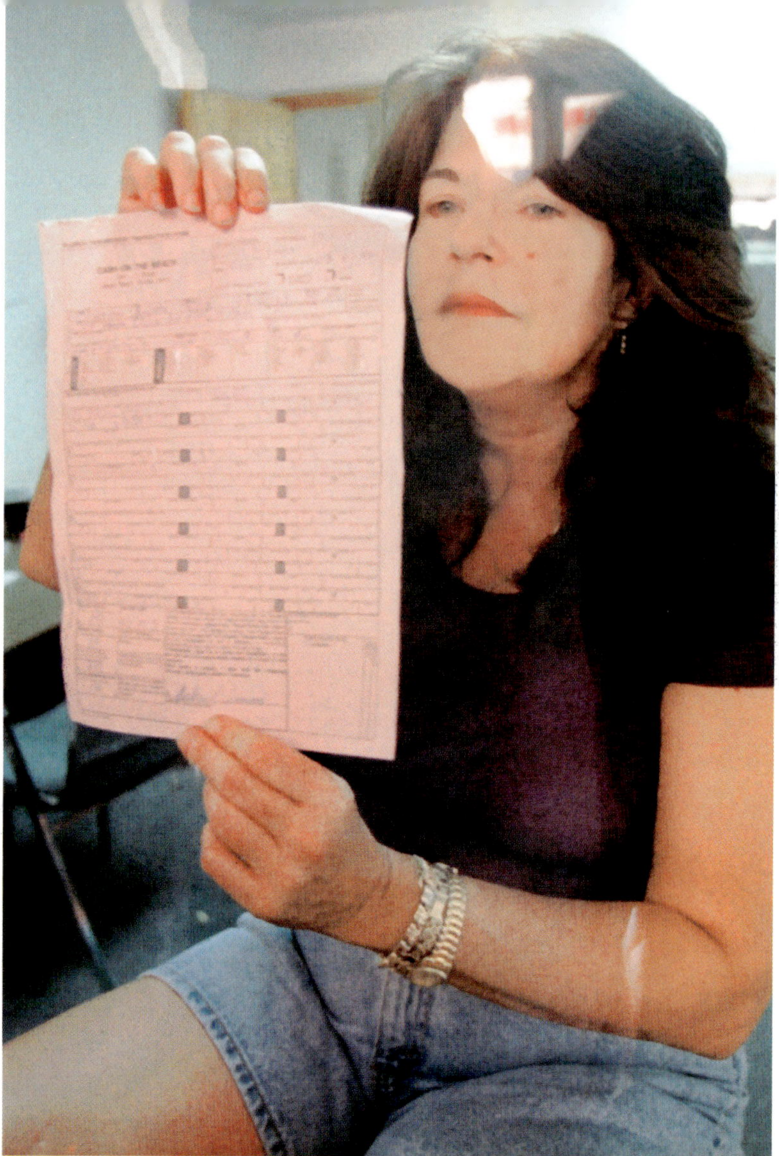

Oliva told police that Cunanan didn't look like a killer. She said that he seemed calm during his visit to the pawn shop. Oliva was photographed holding Cunanan's signed form behind the pawn shop window.

work on the day Versace was killed, the murder investigation took precedence over filing pawn shop forms.

Once the form was found, police realized they had proof that a suspected murderer had been in the area since at least July 10. They also had a local address for Cunanan at the Normandy Plaza Hotel. On the evening of July 16, 30 officers arrived at the hotel to search for Cunanan.[3] Hotel manager Hernandez, along with hotel staff and residents, said they didn't recognize Cunanan's name or photo. Cunanan had registered under a different name. In addition, the room number listed on the pawn shop form was occupied by someone else. Police staked out the pawn shop in case Cunanan returned to claim the coin.

The next day, Hernandez remembered Cunanan and called police to let them know that the criminal had been in room 322. Miami Beach police returned to search the room. Police had not searched the room earlier because their search warrant applied only to rooms that were occupied, and room 322 was empty. In the room, officers dusted for fingerprints and collected items Cunanan had left behind, including books, magazines, and a pair of hair scissors.

TAINTED EVIDENCE

Before the police searched Cunanan's room in the Normandy Plaza Hotel, they didn't know that a hotel employee had let a crime reporter from a Chicago TV station into the room. The reporter had handled and photographed items in the room. When the police learned this, they were furious. Because the reporter had touched things in the room, all fingerprints and evidence were now compromised. If critical evidence, such as the murder weapon, had been found in the room, it may not have been admissible as evidence in court.

Linking Murders

The Miami Beach Police Department focused its efforts on apprehending Cunanan for the murder of Versace. At the same time, law enforcement agencies in Minnesota, Chicago, and New Jersey were eager to catch and question Cunanan about the murders that took place in their jurisdictions.

The FBI and local police continued to gather physical evidence that linked Cunanan to the murders of Versace, Reese, Miglin, Madson, and Trail. The different vehicles Cunanan used provided significant evidence. In addition to Cunanan's passport, police recovered the insurance certificate to Miglin's Lexus and Reese's Social Security card. Numerous pieces of incriminating evidence were also found in Miglin's Lexus, including the photo of Cunanan's friends and the items used in Miglin's murder.

The thumbprint from the pawn shop fingerprint card matched the one on Cunanan's driver's license. The FBI also discovered that gold coins had been stolen from Miglin's home when he was murdered. The gold coin pawned by Cunanan matched the coins stolen from Miglin.

The New Jersey State Police eventually matched Cunanan's fingerprint to one found on the inside of a back door handle in Miglin's Lexus.

The most compelling pieces of evidence were the bullet casings found

BALLISTICS ANALYSIS

Ballistics is a field of forensic science that involves the examination of guns used to commit crimes. Bullets are made out of soft metal, while metal gun barrels are hard. As a result, bullets get scraped and nicked as they are loaded and fired. Ballistics experts analyze the bullets under powerful microscopes. If two bullets have the same markings, experts can conclude that they were fired by the same gun. Ballistics experts can also fire a bullet from a gun and compare the bullet markings to those found at a crime scene to identify the murder weapon. Ballistics evidence can be used in court to tie a weapon—and its owner—to crimes.

near the bodies of Versace, Reese, and Madson. The casings recovered at the Versace murder site were immediately hand-delivered to an FBI forensics lab in Washington, DC, where they were compared to the casings from the other murder investigations.

By the next day, ballistics experts concluded without a doubt that the same .40 caliber gun used to kill Versace had been used to kill Madson and Reese. The bullets were the same kind found in the black nylon bag. The one important piece of evidence the authorities didn't have, however, was the actual gun used to carry out the murders.

A Failed Manhunt

On July 18, a memorial service was held for Versace at Saint Patrick Catholic Church in Miami. Undercover police officers and FBI agents blended into the large crowd. They hoped to catch a glimpse of Cunanan among the mourners.

Hundreds of people attended the memorial service for Versace at Saint Patrick Catholic Church. Police officers were stationed both inside and outside the church in case Cunanan decided to attend the service.

They thought Cunanan might be confident or arrogant enough to taunt police by attending his victim's funeral. It was now three days after Versace's murder, and there was still no sign of Cunanan. The authorities didn't appear to have any leads.

Thousands of law enforcement officers had spent more than two months searching for Cunanan. It was threatening to become what journalist Maureen Orth called the largest failed manhunt in US history. She went on to write a book about the case, noting that this "nationwide manhunt that cost millions yielded little result."[4]

CHAPTER SEVEN

THE SEARCH ENDS

The FBI and local law enforcement agencies knew that Cunanan's pattern was to kill, steal the victim's vehicle, and move on quickly. This meant that Cunanan could be anywhere. But the fact that Cunanan had left behind Reese's truck—his current getaway vehicle—gave the authorities hope that he was still in the South Florida area. The police knew they needed to find Cunanan quickly, before he had the chance to strike again.

The Houseboat

Fernando Carreira had a business looking after properties in Miami Beach. On July 23, Carreira and his wife stopped a little before 4:00 p.m. for a routine check on a property. It was a blue two-story houseboat anchored at 5250 Collins Avenue

The 3,000-square-foot (278 sq m) houseboat where Cunanan hid was located in a popular oceanfront area known for its hotels, boats, and boutiques.

When Cunanan was found, he had been officially charged with the murders of Madson, Reese, and Miglin but not yet the murders of Trail and Versace.

on Indian Creek, about two miles (3 km) north of Versace's mansion.[1]

The houseboat's owner lived in Las Vegas, Nevada, and the houseboat had been empty since the end of December. When Carreira reached the houseboat, he immediately noticed that the top lock on the front door was jammed or broken. The bottom lock was unlatched. That was not the way Carreira had left it the last time he checked on the houseboat. Right away, he suspected that an intruder might be on the premises. He pulled out a gun for protection as he entered the houseboat.

As he walked through the front door, Carreira saw that all the lights were on. The drapes were drawn too, although he always left them open. Carreira walked into the living room and saw that the couch cushions had been pulled down and

REWARD MONEY

During the manhunt, a number of organizations offered reward money for Cunanan's capture. Carreira collected a total of $55,000 from several entities, including the FBI, the New York City Anti-Violence Project, the Miami Beach Police Department, and the Greater Miami Convention and Visitors Bureau. Not everyone agreed that Carreira deserved the reward money, since he didn't actually capture Cunanan. But Carreira defended his role, saying, "Because of me, they found him."[2]

arranged like a bed on the floor. A pair of sandals he'd never seen before were in the room. He was about to continue his search when a loud bang rang out on the second floor. Carreira ran out of the houseboat, fearing that someone had shot at him. He told his wife to keep an eye on the houseboat from a safe distance while he called the police. He was so nervous that he had to get his son to dial 911 for him.

No Escape

The police arrived at the houseboat within four minutes.[3] They were on high alert to capture Cunanan and were taking no chances that the houseboat intruder might be him. The police ordered a shutdown of all traffic on Collins Avenue in an effort to keep the area clear. Police officers surrounded the houseboat, helicopters hovered overhead, and police boats patrolled the water. The Miami Beach Police called in Miami-Dade's Special Response Team (SRT) for additional help. Officers in the SRT were specially trained to respond to dangerous situations and handle negotiations.

Despite the authorities' best efforts to secure the area, chaos ensued over the next few hours. With traffic on Collins Avenue detoured, many residents couldn't reach their homes. Some people tried to walk through the area. Residents in the luxury high-rise apartment buildings and tourists staying in hotels along Collins Avenue stood on their balconies to see what was going on. Reporters and television crews arrived. Police knew that whoever was in the houseboat was armed, so they tried to keep people out of the line of fire.

Police used a bullhorn to try to communicate with the suspect in the houseboat and persuade him to come out peacefully. "Andrew, come out, the whole world is watching!" officers yelled through the bullhorn.[4] At one point, they threw a phone into the houseboat and instructed the suspect to pick it up and talk to them. For about five hours, police tried to communicate with the suspect, but they received no response.[5]

At 8:00 p.m., the SRT lobbed canisters of tear gas into the houseboat in an attempt to force the suspect out. Police tried one more time to talk with him but still received no answer. They finally decided it was time to go inside the houseboat.

Suicide

At 8:20 p.m., a team of SRT officers entered the houseboat. First, they searched the main floor but found no one hiding there. Then they headed carefully to the second floor, where they discovered a man's body in the master bedroom. He was propped on a pillow soaked in a pool of blood. He was dead from a gunshot to his head, and the gun was in his hand, resting on his stomach. His eyes were open, and several days' worth of stubble covered his chin. The man appeared to have died by suicide. According to police reports, the suspect was cold to the touch and had already been dead for several hours. Police officers recovered a single bullet casing lying next to a sliding glass window. Police assumed they had finally found Cunanan, but they needed forensic experts to make sure it was him.

Miami Herald newspaper reporters nicknamed the houseboat where Cunanan hid the "Houseboat of Horrors."[6]

Police technicians arrived at the houseboat after midnight to collect forensic evidence and identify the body. First, they carefully removed the gun from the dead man's hand and wrote down the weapon's serial number. They matched the body's thumbprint to the one on record for Cunanan. By the morning of July 24, they had confirmed that the

More than 100 police officers and FBI agents surrounded the houseboat after Carreira reported the break-in. They swarmed around the houseboat on foot, on boats, and even in helicopters.

When officers found Cunanan, they said the killer looked very thin and was dressed only in boxer shorts. Newspaper stories about the Versace case were found near the body. Officers carried Cunanan's body out of the houseboat in a blue body bag.

body was Andrew Cunanan's. The serial number on the gun matched the one used to murder Madson, Reese, and Versace. The two-month manhunt for Cunanan was finally over. The authorities had Cunanan's body and the murder weapon. But what they didn't have was a suicide note.

Questions Remain

A suicide note could have helped answer the many questions investigators had about Cunanan, his motives, and his movements in Miami Beach. The big question that remained for police was why Cunanan had killed Versace. Had he come to Miami Beach with the intention of killing Versace? And if so, how long had he been planning the murder?

It was also possible that Cunanan came to Miami Beach for an entirely different reason. His killing of Versace might have been unplanned. Over the next few months, detectives and other experts pored over the evidence to try to uncover a motive for Cunanan's killing spree.

Investigators wondered why Cunanan had stayed in Miami Beach after murdering Versace. In the past, Cunanan had killed, stolen his victims' cars, and moved on. But with Versace's murder, Cunanan broke his pattern and stayed hidden just blocks away from the scene of his crime. In addition, Cunanan left behind Reese's truck with his passport inside. As a result, he didn't have the means to easily leave the country or even the local area.

IDENTIFYING THE BODY

Forensic experts worked through the night to identify Cunanan's body. After removing the gun from Cunanan's hand, they swabbed the gunpowder burns between his fingers. From this evidence, technicians could tell that Cunanan had pulled the trigger on the gun to kill himself. They used magnifying glasses to carefully scrutinize the pad of Cunanan's right thumb. They compared every loop, whorl, and arch to the thumbprints on the pawn shop form and on Cunanan's California driver's license. On the morning of July 24, they declared the prints a match.

The intense pressure of the manhunt may have led Cunanan to lie low. He likely recognized that it would be difficult to make a move without getting caught. But it seemed as if Cunanan had not given up hope of an escape. According to police records, Cunanan made a call a few days after Versace's murder. He called someone he knew on the West Coast in hopes of obtaining a fake passport and leaving the United States.

When that plan fell through, Cunanan may have thought that he'd run out of options. Then came the sound of someone entering his hideout. He must have known he would soon be found, possibly by the police. Perhaps he gave up at that point. Or Cunanan might have believed that there was only one way to stay in control of the situation: to take his own life, taking the story of his murder spree with him.

HOUSEBOAT CONNECTION

The houseboat where Cunanan hid was owned by Torsten Reineck, a German national who lived in Las Vegas, Nevada. Miami authorities began investigating a possible connection between Reineck, Versace, and Cunanan. Some investigators didn't believe that Cunanan was in that particular houseboat by chance and thought that someone may have helped him hide there. Reineck insisted that he did not know Cunanan. But the suicide of Versace's murderer in his houseboat brought unwanted attention to Reineck, who was wanted in Germany for tax evasion.

CUNANAN IN MIAMI BEACH

Cunanan hid in different locations during his time in Miami Beach, including a hotel and a houseboat. Before and after Versace's murder, Cunanan was also spotted in several locations in the area.

CHAPTER EIGHT

UNKNOWN MOTIVES

When Cunanan died by suicide, he took the truth about why he killed Versace and the other victims with him. Without a suicide note or the ability to interview the murderer, police had to try to piece together a motive based on evidence, witness accounts, and interviews with family and friends of Cunanan and the victims. They also relied on insights from experts who studied the psychology of murderers.

Why Did Cunanan Kill?

The murders of Trail and Madson led police to speculate on a straightforward motive. Trail, Madson, and Cunanan were friends, and Cunanan was known to have had romantic attachments to Madson. The police suspected jealousy or anger as a motive. Friends reported that Cunanan had been in love

After Cunanan's body was discovered in the houseboat, Barreto spoke at press conferences to give updates and answer questions about the case.

WJNO

with Madson, who had a new boyfriend. Trail's sister also told police that Cunanan had always been jealous of Trail having other friends.

Police interviews with friends of Trail and Cunanan revealed that the two men could have had a falling out over drugs. Some of Cunanan's acquaintances reported that he may have started dealing prescription and illegal drugs to finance his lifestyle after he lost his last wealthy boyfriend. Cunanan had been spending lots of money before he left San Diego and was heavily in debt. Police believe he might have tried to persuade Trail to help him deal drugs. Friends said that Trail did not approve of Cunanan selling drugs and that Cunanan might have gotten angry when Trail refused or criticized him.

Cunanan owed more than $40,000 on his credit cards when he left for Minneapolis.[1]

However, these theories became complicated as the number of Cunanan's victims mounted. Since the killings included people who were apparently unknown to Cunanan, police had a more difficult time understanding what sparked the string of killings and how the murders were connected. Some acquaintances interviewed by police said that in addition to dealing drugs, Cunanan had become addicted to crack cocaine and methamphetamines. Both drugs can result in extremely violent and unpredictable behavior. If Cunanan was a user of these drugs, it could explain why he had gone on a murder spree.

THE AIDS THEORY

One suggested motive for Versace's murder was that he had given Cunanan HIV, the virus that causes AIDS. A way to prove that theory was to test Cunanan's and Versace's DNA for the virus. DNA, or deoxyribonucleic acid, is a chemical that is the basis of genetics. Various traits are passed from parent to child through DNA. Shortly after Cunanan's death, though, a medical examiner accidentally made public the fact that Cunanan's autopsy showed he had not had HIV.

Some psychologists and criminologists suggested that Cunanan might have been taking revenge on members of the gay community for some reason. For example, Cunanan may have been dumped by a boyfriend or lover. This could have led him to take his anger out on the entire gay community. However, some people questioned the likelihood of this motive. They pointed out that two of Cunanan's victims were married to women and were not known to have had relationships with men.

Why Versace?

The FBI and police also considered various motives for Cunanan's murder of Versace. Was Versace's murder a random act of violence, or did Cunanan specifically target the fashion designer? Was Versace a stranger to Cunanan, or did the two men know each other? Shortly after Versace's murder, Detective

The News Cafe was reportedly Versace's favorite café in Miami Beach. He visited regularly to buy breakfast, coffee, and magazines. On the morning of Versace's murder, staff at the café noted that the designer appeared to be in more of a hurry than usual.

Scrimshaw developed four possible motives: a Mafia hit, robbery, revenge for acquiring HIV, or a completely random act of violence.

The theory that the killing was related to the Mafia was quickly disregarded when Cunanan became the main suspect. It's possible that the murder was completely random. Cunanan may have been continuing his string of killings, and Versace was just in the wrong place at the wrong time. As for the robbery motive, some witnesses reported that Cunanan quickly approached Versace, shot him, and walked away. But other witnesses said the two men appeared to struggle over a bag before the shooting. Perhaps Cunanan saw Versace and suddenly decided to rob him.

Or, there's some evidence that Cunanan followed Versace that morning, perhaps planning to rob or kill him for another reason. Some witnesses told police that Versace took an unusual route to the News Cafe that morning. Stephanie Vanover, the hostess of the café, reported that Versace "walked past the entrance, circled back around and then went in. It's almost as though he knew someone was following him."[2]

But robbery didn't seem like a likely motive, since Cunanan did not take anything from Versace. And if the killing was random, it seemed coincidental that Cunanan chose to spend two months in Miami Beach without harming anyone and then murdered Versace less than a week after the designer returned to town. This led many authorities to believe that Cunanan came to Miami Beach to kill Versace for some reason. Chief Barreto suspected some sort of link between the two men. "Cunanan picked Versace for a reason," he said. "Maybe they knew each other, or maybe Versace was part of Cunanan's fantasy life and he was rejected by him, and then he retaliated."[3]

FANTASY LIFE

Perhaps ashamed of his middle-class suburban upbringing, Cunanan was fond of making up stories about a much more glamorous life. He often went by aliases and bragged that he came from great wealth. Sometimes he bragged that he came from a royal family in the Philippines and that his father was a Filipino military general. Other times he boasted that his father was a Hollywood executive, that his family owned a factory in Mexico, or that he was part of a prominent Jewish family from Israel.

One possible reason for killing Versace could be a desire to be famous. For some serial killers, fame is a motivation. Cunanan was reportedly someone who craved the limelight. Friends from Cunanan's childhood and adulthood described him as someone who always had to be the center of attention. According to one friend, Cunanan "was always a loud kid, very boisterous."[4] Killing an internationally known celebrity would be one way for Cunanan to gain worldwide attention.

Evidence also suggests that Cunanan may have been jealous of or obsessed with Versace. The designer may have been an example of everything that Cunanan strove for but couldn't achieve: he was an openly gay man who was successful, wealthy, and loved. Cunanan could have been acting out of extreme jealousy. The FBI

Cunanan's senior high school class voted him the student most likely to be remembered.

Versace was a successful man known for his iconic, glamorous designs. Many people wondered if Cunanan targeted Versace because he thought killing a celebrity would make him famous.

interviewed friends and acquaintances of Cunanan's who said he often spoke about Versace, wore Versace label underwear, and even bragged about knowing the designer. But friends also said Cunanan was known to make up stories about his life to hide the truth about himself.

A Possible Meeting?

A personal connection to Versace, however, could be more than one of Cunanan's tall tales. Cunanan and Versace may have met in San Francisco in 1990. Versace and D'Amico were in the city for the opening of an opera for which Versace had designed the costumes. While in San Francisco, Versace visited local bars and nightclubs.

One night, both Versace and Cunanan were at a nightclub called Colossus. According to some witnesses, Versace walked up to Cunanan and said he thought he knew him from Lake Como in Italy, where Versace had a home. Cunanan responded that they had met and thanked Versace for remembering him. But D'Amico always maintained that Versace and Cunanan had never met.

Identifying a Pattern

During and after the investigation, authorities sought to determine a pattern for Cunanan's killings. Doing so could help explain the reason behind the killings or predict potential future victims. Over the course of about three months, Cunanan killed five men, but he didn't kill all of them in the same way. First, he killed two close friends in Minneapolis. One was bludgeoned and one was shot. Then Cunanan killed three apparent strangers. He tortured a man to death in Chicago, then shot a man in New Jersey. Finally, he shot Versace in what seemed to be a random act of violence.

At first, Cunanan appeared to be on a killing spree. A spree killer generally murders multiple people at two or more locations at a relatively fast pace. The killer doesn't take a break

CUNANAN'S VICTIMS

VICTIM	DATE KILLED	DATE FOUND	LOCATION	MURDER WEAPON
Jeffrey Trail, 28	April 27	April 29	Minneapolis, MN, in the apartment of David Madson	Hammer
David Madson, 33	May 2 (or earlier)	May 3	Chisago County, MN, on the shore of East Rush Lake	.40 caliber handgun
Lee Miglin, 75	May 3 or May 4	May 4	Chicago, IL, in the garage of the Miglin home	Screwdriver and other implements
William Reese, 45	May 9	May 9	Pennsville, NJ, in the basement of the cemetery office	.40 caliber handgun
Gianni Versace, 50	July 15	July 15	Miami Beach, FL, at the front gate of the Versace villa	.40 caliber handgun

Cunanan murdered five men in different places and in different ways. While he knew two of his victims, some of the other killings appeared random. Investigators are still unsure about Cunanan's motives.

between murders. Some people describe spree killings as a rampage. According to a report by the FBI's National Center for the Analysis of Violent Crime, spree killings are usually the result of one precipitating event. At one point during the investigation, one witness suggested that the event that set off the spree might have been Cunanan's discovery that he had HIV. But this turned out to be false when an autopsy concluded that Cunanan did not have HIV.

Cunanan killed his first four victims quickly, one after the other, between April 27 and May 9. Then Cunanan waited more than two months before killing Versace. Multiple murders separated by a cooling-off period is the hallmark of a serial killer. The cooling-off period can be days, weeks, or months. It allows the serial killer to methodically plan the next murder. The FBI determined that Cunanan best fit the definition of a serial killer. One FBI expert concluded that Cunanan began as

A DIFFICULT CHILDHOOD

In 1990, a study concluded that most serial killers had one factor in common: a problematic home environment during childhood. This may include substance abuse, emotional neglect, or a lack of parental involvement. Cunanan was an extremely bright child who received a lot of attention from his parents. But his parents' marriage was unhappy. When Cunanan was 19 years old, his father was accused of fraud and abandoned the family. They were left to survive on food stamps and welfare. This family conflict and financial instability may have impacted Cunanan's later behavior, especially his desire to be wealthy.

a spree killer and then evolved into a serial killer.

Cunanan sometimes used the alias Count Ashkenazy.

Serial killers murder for a variety of reasons, such as anger or thrill seeking. Some serial killers don't want to draw attention to themselves, which allows them to continue killing. Others enjoy their celebrity status and want to be noticed. They may choose celebrities as victims. Or they might flirt with capture by killing in public places and leaving obvious clues behind for the police.

Cunanan seemed to fit the attention-seeking type of serial killer. His final victim was a famous person whom he killed in front of witnesses. And throughout his string of murders, Cunanan intentionally left behind evidence, such as weapons, photos, and identification. Captain Tom Cronin of the Chicago Police Department said, "One of the things that strikes me is that he purposely leaves a trail—connect the dots, find me. It's his ego saying, 'I don't want to not get credit.'"[5]

Identifying a pattern for Cunanan's choice of victims would be one way to help establish motive. But doing so was not easy. Trail, Madson, and Versace were all gay, which could suggest a pattern. These three victims were all successful men, which could also be a pattern. Another possibility is that all the victims were men who Cunanan had wanted to have relationships with or men he had desired but knew he could never have.

Some people investigated Cunanan's past for clues about what might have led to his serial killer behavior. Some noted that for his high school yearbook quote, Cunanan chose the ominous phrase *Après moi, le déluge,* which means "After me, the flood."

Miglin didn't fit a pattern as neatly as Trail, Madson, and Versace did. Miglin was a married man with children. His family insisted that he was not gay and did not know Cunanan. Therefore, they argue that he could not have been one of Cunanan's older wealthy boyfriends. The police officially declared Miglin's murder as random, but that didn't make sense to some serial killer psychology experts.

The extended torture and beating of Miglin's face suggested that the crime was personal. In addition, Cunanan did not need to break into Miglin's home and apparently felt comfortable enough to spend the night in the house. This could have indicated that Cunanan may have known Miglin and been familiar with his home. Experts also noted that Cunanan had beaten Trail's face with a hammer and shot Versace in the face. According to William Hagmaier, who was in charge of the FBI's Child Abduction and Serial Killer Unit, this focus on faces seemed to point to a personal connection with the victims.

The other victim who did not fit into any obvious pattern is Reese. His murder may have been what serial killer experts call a functional homicide. Cunanan needed a car to replace the Lexus, which he knew police officers were tracking. He may have killed Reese simply in order to steal his truck.

The murders committed by Cunanan might have been a combination of random, spree, and serial killings without a single motive. Cunanan may have had multiple motives, killing friends and strangers for different reasons. "For all I know, this violence came out of the blue," said Sergeant Tichich.[6] In the end, all the evidence, interviews, and expert testimony can shed light on possible motives. But the real reason why Cunanan killed Versace—or anyone else—remains unknown.

CHAPTER NINE

CASE CLOSED

At the end of December 1997, the Miami Beach Police Department issued a final report on the Versace murder investigation. The report filled three plastic binders with 700 pages of documented evidence and more than 1,000 photos. It included crime scene photos of Reese's truck, the houseboat, the blood-soaked pillow that Cunanan's head had rested on, and the bloody shorts Versace had been wearing when he was shot. The report also included 13 videotapes and 17 audiotapes of interviews and crime scene footage.[1] The release of the report signaled the official closing of the case.

No Surprises

Despite the report's comprehensiveness, it contained little new information about Versace's murder and the overall investigation. The report detailed the fingerprints and physical evidence that linked Cunanan to the murders of Trail, Madson,

Versace's villa is a popular tourist spot. Many people snap selfies or photos on the front steps. The villa also features a high-end restaurant and bar.

POLICE REVIEW

After the Versace murder investigation concluded, the office of the Miami Beach City Manager issued a review of the police department's handling of the case. In general, the report concluded that the investigation had been well handled by police, but it noted that there were some weaknesses that needed to be addressed. As a result, the Miami Beach Police Department switched to a computerized system for pawn shop forms, allowing immediate access to that information. The Thirteenth Street parking garage policy also changed so that vehicles needed a new ticket every day. This helped ensure that stolen vehicles involved in crimes could not be hidden in the parking garage.

Miglin, Reese, and Versace. The most important piece of evidence was the gun found with Cunanan's body and the matching bullet casings at the murder scenes of Madson, Reese, and Versace.

The gun and bullets stood out to investigators because they were an unusual choice for a murder weapon. A .40 caliber handgun is very heavy and powerful. Also, Cunanan used Golden Saber bullets, which turn into mushroom shapes when fired into a target. This inflicts a great deal of damage. These types of gun and bullets are both much deadlier than necessary for a murder weapon.

The final report was not able to shed any light on a motive for Versace's murder. Investigators interviewed many people who knew Cunanan and Versace, but they found no clear evidence that the two men knew each other or had met. According to the report, the only firm link between the two men was that they were both openly gay and part of gay communities.

The report noted that it was possible Cunanan and Versace crossed paths at some point at a bar or nightclub that catered to gay men. The report also included testimony from D'Amico that he and Versace occasionally hired male prostitutes, and acquaintances reported that Cunanan worked as a prostitute. But D'Amico said he had never seen Cunanan before and had never seen him with Versace.

There was no concrete evidence that the men met in San Francisco or elsewhere. Versace's sister, Donatella, said, "I am sure my brother never met him."[2] One Miami Beach detective remained unconvinced. "My gut says yes, that there was a connection between these two," he said. "I wish we could have kept the investigation open until we knew for sure."[3] Chief Barreto said there was no way to know Cunanan's exact motives. "We can speculate about the motive being robbery, or Andrew Cunanan going out in a big way, or revenge for some perceived act by Versace," he said. "But unfortunately, the real answer went down with the ship, so to speak, when Andrew Cunanan committed suicide."[4]

There was also no evidence tying Cunanan to Reineck, the owner of the houseboat. Police investigated leads that would connect Cunanan or Versace with organized crime too. But they found no evidence to support these theories.

The report did contain details of the only eyewitness account of Versace's murder, as told by his neighbor Mersiha Colakovic. According to her witness statement, Colakovic had noticed a man who seemed to be waiting for Versace, but she thought he must have been a friend or fan of Versace's. After the shooting, she saw Cunanan place the gun in his bag and walk calmly down Ocean Drive as if nothing had happened.

Unanswered Questions

The final report could not answer some of the questions that had puzzled police throughout the investigation. Without a suicide note, there was no solid evidence about why Cunanan had embarked on the killing spree. With no concrete evidence to connect Cunanan and Versace, the motive for the designer's murder remains unknown. Detective Scrimshaw said clear proof that Cunanan and Versace knew each other "would have made sense of the whole thing."[5]

Another unanswered question was whether Madson had been involved in Trail's murder. The discovery of the bloody size 36 jeans provided evidence that Cunanan had most likely bludgeoned Trail. But police didn't know if Madson was present during the killing, which would have made him an accomplice to the murder. If the medical examiner was correct that Cunanan had killed Madson on May 2, it would mean that the two men had spent five days together after Trail's murder.

Versace's sister, Donatella, *center*, and the rest of the Versace family firmly believed that Gianni had never met Cunanan. Donatella was close with her brother and said that when he was killed, it felt like her world fell apart.

What had they done during that time? Had Madson stayed with Cunanan willingly, or had Cunanan had some way of keeping Madson close? And whether or not Madson was an accomplice in Trail's murder, why had Cunanan killed Madson?

It is possible that the estimated time of Madson's death was incorrect and he had been killed days earlier than May 2. That would explain the parking ticket that placed Madson's Jeep in Chicago on April 30 even though Madson was killed in Minnesota. Madson's family and friends worked hard to clear Madson's name as an accomplice in Trail's murder. On June 16, 1998, more than a year after Trail's and Madson's deaths, the Minneapolis Police Department called a press conference to announce that there was no evidence to implicate Madson in Trail's murder.

Versace stores are located all over the world. Under Donatella's creative leadership, the brand has grown to include not only fashions based on her brother's designs but also new styles inspired by Donatella's own tastes.

Versace's Legacy

At the time of Versace's death, 130 of his shops around the world sold designer clothes as well as linen, perfume, and other accessories. A Versace dress could fetch as much as $11,600. The company also had a chain of 50 stores that sold less expensive clothing under the Versus line.[6]

The entire company was privately owned by the Versace family. Gianni owned the biggest share of the company, 45 percent. His brother, Santo, owned 35 percent and was the company's CEO. His sister, Donatella, who was his closest working partner, owned 20 percent.[7] In his will, Versace left his controlling share of the company to his 11-year-old niece, Allegra. After her brother's death, Donatella became the new designer of the House of Versace, and the family vowed to keep Versace's legacy flourishing.

In December 1997, just five months after Versace's death, a major retrospective of his work opened at the Costume Institute of the Metropolitan Museum of Art in New York City.

In 2018, the company was sold to Michael Kors for $2.1 billion, although Donatella continued to serve as the brand's head designer.[8] Versace fashions for men, women, and children continue to sell worldwide. Donatella's fall 2023 ready-to-wear women's clothing collection was showcased in a fashion show in Los Angeles. Many celebrities attended the show, including Cher, Elton John, Kendall Jenner, and Anne Hathaway.

For many years after Versace's murder, tourists in Miami Beach visited and took pictures at the villa, Normandy Plaza

FINAL FASHION SHOW

Twice a year, Milan Fashion Week is held in Milan, Italy. It features shows by major fashion designers and draws an international audience. It is one of the most important fashion events in the world. During the October 1997 Milan Fashion Week, the Versace fashion show went on as planned just three months after Versace's death. Celebrities such as Cher, Boy George, and Demi Moore attended the show. Rival fashion designers Armani, Donna Karan, Miuccia Prada, and Karl Lagerfeld also attended to show their support.

Versace's mansion later became a luxury boutique hotel called the Villa Casa Casuarina.

Hotel, and other sites related to the crime. Versace's memory has also been kept alive through books, television shows, and movies exploring his life and death.

When Versace was murdered, journalist Maureen Orth was working on a story about Cunanan's murder spree for *Vanity Fair* magazine. After completing the article, Orth wrote a book about the investigation. It was titled *Vulgar Favors* and

In 2019, actor Darren Criss, *left*, won a Golden Globe award for his role as Andrew Cunanan in *The Assassination of Gianni Versace*. Director Ryan Murphy, *right*, accepted the award for best limited series.

published in 1999. While researching for the book, Orth used interviews from more than 400 people and thousands of pages of police reports.[9]

The book was used as inspiration for *The Assassination of Gianni Versace*, which aired as part of FX's *American Crime Story* series in 2018. The nine-episode television show was directed by the award-winning Ryan Murphy. It starred Penélope Cruz as Donatella, Ricky Martin as D'Amico, Édgar Ramírez as Versace, and Darren Criss as Cunanan.

If Cunanan was looking for the limelight, he succeeded. He lives on in infamy as the man who killed a world-famous fashion designer in what remains a puzzling crime. Cunanan may have embarked on his murder spree with the intent to kill Versace. Or perhaps Versace simply stumbled into the path of a brutal serial killer.

FACTS OR FANTASY?

According to FX, the network behind *The Assassination of Gianni Versace*, the series was inspired by true events. But both the Versace family and Versace's partner, D'Amico, were unhappy with the show. The Versace family issued a statement that the series should be considered fiction. D'Amico said the show included many inaccurate and misleading scenes, particularly a scene in which Versace and Cunanan meet in San Francisco. D'Amico said that it was "pure fantasy."[10]

TIMELINE

1997

- On April 25, Andrew Cunanan flies from San Diego, California, to Minneapolis, Minnesota, to visit his friends Jeffrey Trail and David Madson.
- On April 27, Trail is bludgeoned to death by Cunanan.
- On April 29, a body is found rolled up in a carpet in Madson's apartment. The police assume the body is Madson's.
- On April 30, the body in the carpet is identified as Trail's. Madson is suspected of Trail's murder. On that same day, Cunanan may have parked Madson's Jeep in a parking garage in Chicago.
- On May 3, Madson's body is found by two fishermen on the shore of East Rush Lake outside Minneapolis. Madson's Jeep is missing. Sometime either this day or on May 4, Lee Miglin is tortured to death at his home in Chicago.
- On May 4, a criminal advisory is issued for Cunanan. Miglin's body is found in his garage. His Lexus is missing.
- On May 7, a police officer notices Madson's Jeep parked around the corner from Miglin's home. The FBI becomes involved in the investigation and search for Cunanan.
- On May 9, William Reese is killed at a cemetery in Pennsville, New Jersey. Miglin's Lexus is left at the site, and Reese's red truck is missing.
- On May 10, *America's Most Wanted* features Cunanan.
- On May 12, Cunanan checks into the Normandy Plaza Hotel in Miami Beach, Florida, under an alias.
- On June 12, the FBI adds Cunanan to its Ten Most Wanted Fugitives list.
- On July 7, Cunanan pawns a gold coin and gives the pawn shop owner his name and identification. The paperwork is provided to the Miami Beach Police Department.
- On July 10, Gianni Versace arrives at his villa in Miami Beach. That same day, a sandwich shop employee recognizes Cunanan and alerts police.

- On July 15, Cunanan shoots Versace on the steps of his villa and walks away without getting caught. Later that night, the Miami Beach Police Department names Cunanan as the suspect in Versace's murder.
- On July 16, the pawn shop owner recognizes Cunanan as the man who pawned the gold coin. She calls police, who discover the forms she had submitted on July 7.
- On July 23, a caretaker discovers evidence of an intruder in a Miami Beach houseboat and calls police. After five hours, police enter the houseboat and find Cunanan dead by suicide.
- In December, the final report on the investigation is released. The case is closed without establishing a motive for Versace's murder.

1999

- *Vulgar Favors: Andrew Cunanan, Gianni Versace, and the Largest Failed Manhunt in U.S. History* by Maureen Orth is published.

2018

- On January 17, the nine-episode series *The Assassination of Gianni Versace* airs on FX.
- In September, the fashion empire founded by Versace in 1978 is sold to Michael Kors.

2022

- In November, Versace's former Miami Beach home opens to guests as the Villa Casa Casuarina.

ESSENTIAL FACTS

SIGNIFICANT EVENTS

- In April 1997, Andrew Cunanan begins a murder spree by killing two of his friends in Minneapolis, Minnesota. He bludgeons Jeffrey Trail to death on April 27. Days later, he shoots and kills David Madson.
- On May 3 or May 4, Cunanan tortures and kills Chicago businessman Lee Miglin. He stays the night in Miglin's home before driving away in Miglin's Lexus.
- On May 9, Cunanan shoots and kills William Reese, a cemetery caretaker, in a remote location in New Jersey and steals his truck.
- On July 15, Cunanan walks up to Gianni Versace on the steps of his villa in Miami Beach, Florida, and shoots him twice before calmly walking away and disappearing from sight. Versace is rushed to the hospital and pronounced dead.
- On July 23, when it appears that he might be discovered in his hiding place in a Miami Beach houseboat, Cunanan shoots and kills himself. He leaves behind no suicide note or explanation for his string of killings.

KEY PLAYERS

- Andrew Cunanan embarked on a killing spree in 1997 that claimed the lives of five men, the last of whom was Gianni Versace. Cunanan died by suicide just before being caught by authorities.
- Gianni Versace was a world-famous fashion designer who was shot and killed by Cunanan on the steps of his Miami Beach mansion.
- Miami Beach Police detective Paul Scrimshaw was in charge of the Versace murder investigation.
- Minneapolis Police sergeant Bob Tichich investigated the murders of Cunanan's first victims.
- Property caretaker Fernando Carreira discovered Cunanan hiding in a houseboat in Miami Beach and alerted police, which ended the manhunt.

IMPACT ON SOCIETY

In April 1997, 27-year-old Andrew Cunanan embarked on a killing spree, leaving four men dead by mid-May. He killed two of his friends in Minneapolis, Minnesota, He went on to kill two more men who appeared to be complete strangers to him. He left a trail of evidence behind him.

On July 15, Cunanan shocked the world by shooting fashion designer Gianni Versace in broad daylight on the steps of his Miami Beach mansion. Cunanan became the subject of what has been called the largest failed manhunt in US history. Investigators across multiple states worked to discover his whereabouts, posting flyers and notifying members of the public to be on the lookout for Cunanan. The killer died by suicide before being discovered by authorities, taking the mystery of the murders along with him.

During and after the investigation, many people criticized the authorities for not taking the murder spree seriously enough until a celebrity was killed. Others accused law enforcement of prejudice against gay men. They thought the fact that most of Cunanan's victims were gay explained the lackluster response of law enforcement agencies and the FBI. The motive behind the killings remains a mystery. If it was fame that Cunanan was after, he achieved it. Cunanan has been the subject of numerous articles, books, and television shows, and his name will forever be linked with Gianni Versace.

QUOTE

"We can speculate about the motive being robbery, or Andrew Cunanan going out in a big way, or revenge for some perceived act by Versace. But unfortunately, the real answer went down with the ship, so to speak, when Andrew Cunanan committed suicide."

—Miami Beach Police chief Richard Barreto, who was involved in the investigation and search for Cunanan

GLOSSARY

accomplice
Someone who helps a person complete a task. Often used to describe someone who has helped commit a crime.

advisory
An official announcement, typically a warning.

alias
A false name, especially one used by a criminal.

assassin
A person hired to kill a well-known or important person.

autopsy
An examination of a dead body to determine the cause of death.

ballistics
The science of projectiles and firearms.

bulletin
A short official statement or broadcast of news.

caliber
The diameter of the inside of a gun barrel.

casing
In ammunition, the sleeve that contains the gunpowder and bullet.

compromise
To damage or weaken something.

forensic
Characterized by the use of scientific techniques to investigate a crime.

fugitive
A criminal who flees or hides to escape law enforcement.

homicide
The killing of one person by another.

jurisdiction
A certain area within which a group has authority to make a legal decision or take legal action.

magazine
An ammunition storage and feeding device for a repeating firearm.

rampage
A period of violent and uncontrollable behavior.

ADDITIONAL RESOURCES

SELECTED BIBLIOGRAPHY

Ball, Deborah. *House of Versace: The Untold Story of Genius, Murder, and Survival.* Crown Publishers, 2010.

Orth, Maureen. *Vulgar Favors: Andrew Cunanan, Gianni Versace, and the Largest Failed Manhunt in U.S. History.* Delacorte Press, 1999.

"Serial Killers Part 6: Andrew Cunanan Murders a Fashion Icon." *Federal Bureau of Investigation*, 14 Mar. 2014, fbi.gov. Accessed 6 Mar. 2023.

FURTHER READINGS

Cooper, Chris. *Forensic Science*. DK Eyewitness, 2020.

Morris, Rebecca. *The Olympic Park Bombing*. Abdo, 2024.

Newquist, H. P. *Scene of the Crime*. Viking Books, 2021.

ONLINE RESOURCES

Booklinks
NONFICTION NETWORK
FREE! ONLINE NONFICTION RESOURCES

To learn more about Andrew Cunanan and the murder of Gianni Versace, please visit **abdobooklinks.com** or scan this QR code. These links are routinely monitored and updated to provide the most current information available.

MORE INFORMATION

For more information on this subject, contact or visit the following organizations:

AMERICAN ACADEMY OF FORENSIC SCIENCES (AAFS)

410 N. 21st St.
Colorado Springs, CO 80904
aafs.org

The AAFS is a professional society dedicated to promoting forensic science education and improving the accuracy and precision of forensic science.

FEDERAL BUREAU OF INVESTIGATION (FBI)

935 Pennsylvania Ave. NW
Washington, DC 20535
fbi.gov

The FBI is the domestic intelligence and security service of the United States and its principal federal law enforcement agency. It is headquartered in Washington, DC. It played a major role in the manhunt for Cunanan.

VERSACE

20124 Milan
Piazza Luigi Einaudi 4
Italy
versace.com

The Versace fashion design house was founded by Gianni Versace in 1978 in Milan, Italy. It designs, manufactures, and sells clothing, lifestyle products, and accessories.

SOURCE NOTES

CHAPTER 1. MURDER IN MIAMI

1. Rachel Chang. "The Assassination of Gianni Versace: The True Story of His Tragic Death." *Biography*, 10 July 2020, biography.com. Accessed 17 July 2023.

2. Maureen Orth. *Vulgar Favors: Andrew Cunanan, Gianni Versace, and the Largest Failed Manhunt in U.S. History*. Delacorte Press, 1999. 307–308.

3. Orth, *Vulgar Favors*, 346.

4. Chang, "The Assassination of Gianni Versace."

5. Chang, "The Assassination of Gianni Versace."

6. "Murder by Design." *Sun Sentinel*, 16 July 1997, sun-sentinel.com. Accessed 17 July 2023.

7. "Celebrities Stalked by Fear after Versace Slaying." *Deseret News*, 29 July 1997, deseret.com. Accessed 17 July 2023.

CHAPTER 2. AMERICA'S MOST WANTED

1. Rachel Chang. "The Assassination of Gianni Versace: The True Story of His Tragic Death." *Biography*, 10 July 2020, biography.com. Accessed 17 July 2023.

2. Deborah Ball. *House of Versace: The Untold Story of Genius, Murder, and Survival*. Crown Publishers, 2010. 10.

3. Ardy Friedberg, Jay Weaver, and Luisa Yanez. "Versace Murder Case Closed." *Sun Sentinel*, 31 Dec. 1997, sun-sentinel.com. Accessed 17 July 2023.

4. Maureen Orth. *Vulgar Favors: Andrew Cunanan, Gianni Versace, and the Largest Failed Manhunt in U.S. History*. Delacorte Press, 1999. 348.

5. "Murder by Design." *Sun Sentinel*, 16 July 1997, sun-sentinel.com. Accessed 17 July 2023.

CHAPTER 3. MURDER SPREE

1. Maureen Orth. *Vulgar Favors: Andrew Cunanan, Gianni Versace, and the Largest Failed Manhunt in U.S. History*. Delacorte Press, 1999. 189.

2. Orth, *Vulgar Favors*, 187.

3. Orth, *Vulgar Favors*, 211.

4. Orth, *Vulgar Favors*, 239.

CHAPTER 4. GETTING AWAY WITH MURDER

1. Maureen Orth. *Vulgar Favors: Andrew Cunanan, Gianni Versace, and the Largest Failed Manhunt in U.S. History*. Delacorte Press, 1999. 190.

2. Orth, *Vulgar Favors*, 194.

3. Orth, *Vulgar Favors*, 212.

4. Orth, *Vulgar Favors*, 239.

5. Richard Lacayo. "Tagged for Murder." *Time*, 28 July 1997, time.com. Accessed 19 July 2023.

6. Orth, *Vulgar Favors*, 214.

7. Orth, *Vulgar Favors*, 254.

8. Orth, *Vulgar Favors*, 289.

9. Thomas J. Miles. "Estimating the Effect of *America's Most Wanted*: A Duration Analysis of Wanted Fugitives." *Journal of Law and Economics*, vol. 48, no. 1, 2005, 281–306, jstor.org. Accessed 20 July 2023.

10. "Ten Most Wanted Fugitives FAQ." FBI, n.d., fbi.gov. Accessed 20 July 2023.

CHAPTER 5. HIDDEN IN PLAIN SIGHT

1. Maureen Orth. *Vulgar Favors: Andrew Cunanan, Gianni Versace, and the Largest Failed Manhunt in U.S. History*. Delacorte Press, 1999. 301.

2. Rachel Chang. "The Assassination of Gianni Versace: The True Story of His Tragic Death." *Biography*, 10 July 2020, biography.com. Accessed 17 July 2023.

3. Tom Watkins. "Andrew Cunanan's Quiet Life in Miami Beach." *CNN*, 27 July 1997, cnn.com. Accessed 20 July 2023.

4. Maureen Orth. "The Killer's Trail." *Vanity Fair*, 9 Sept. 1997, archive.vanityfair.com. Accessed 20 July 2023.

5. "Ten Most Wanted Fugitives FAQ." *FBI*, n.d., fbi.gov. Accessed 20 July 2023.

6. "Serial Killers Part 6: Andrew Cunanan Murders a Fashion Icon." *FBI*, 14 Mar. 2014, fbi.gov. Accessed 20 July 2023.

7. Orth, *Vulgar Favors*, 318.

SOURCE NOTES CONTINUED

CHAPTER 6. MIAMI MANHUNT

1. Elena Nicolaou. "How Did the Police Track Down Andrew Cunanan?" *Refinery29*, 21 Mar. 2018, refinery29.com. Accessed 20 July 2023.

2. Luisa Yanez. "The Cunanan Mysteries: Why Was Versace a Victim?" *Sun Sentinel*, 12 July 1998, sun-sentinel.com. Accessed 20 July 2023.

3. Maureen Orth. *Vulgar Favors: Andrew Cunanan, Gianni Versace, and the Largest Failed Manhunt in U.S. History*. Delacorte Press, 1999. 368.

4. Orth, *Vulgar Favors*, 4.

CHAPTER 7. THE SEARCH ENDS

1. "Serial Killers Part 6: Andrew Cunanan Murders a Fashion Icon." *FBI*, 14 Mar. 2014, fbi.gov. Accessed 20 July 2023.

2. Maureen Orth. *Vulgar Favors: Andrew Cunanan, Gianni Versace, and the Largest Failed Manhunt in U.S. History*. Delacorte Press, 1999. 426–427.

3. Orth, *Vulgar Favors*, 400.

4. Howard Chua-Eoan. "Dead Men Tell No Tales." *Time*, 24 June 2001, time.com. Accessed 20 July 2023.

5. Johnny Diaz. "20 Years Since Versace's Murder, Caretaker Who Found Suspected Killer Looks Back." *Sun Sentinel*, 4 June 2018, sun-sentinel.com. Accessed 20 July 2023.

6. Orth, *Vulgar Favors*, 426.

CHAPTER 8. UNKNOWN MOTIVES

1. Maureen Orth. *Vulgar Favors: Andrew Cunanan, Gianni Versace, and the Largest Failed Manhunt in U.S. History*. Delacorte Press, 1999. 176.

2. Richard Lacayo. "Tagged for Murder." *Time*, 28 July 1997, time.com. Accessed 19 July 2023.

3. Luisa Yanez. "The Cunanan Mysteries: Why Was Versace a Victim?" *Sun Sentinel*, 12 July 1998, sun-sentinel.com. Accessed 20 July 2023.

4. Orth, *Vulgar Favors*, 22.

5. Orth, *Vulgar Favors*, 295.

6. Maureen Orth. "The Killer's Trail." *Vanity Fair*, 9 Sept. 1997, archive.vanityfair.com. Accessed 20 July 2023.

CHAPTER 9. CASE CLOSED

1. Ardy Friedberg, Jay Weaver, and Luisa Yanez. "Versace Murder Case Closed." *Sun Sentinel*, 31 Dec. 1997, sun-sentinel.com. Accessed 20 July 2023.

2. Maureen Orth. *Vulgar Favors: Andrew Cunanan, Gianni Versace, and the Largest Failed Manhunt in U.S. History*. Delacorte Press, 1999. 434.

3. Luisa Yanez. "The Cunanan Mysteries: Why Was Versace a Victim?" *Sun Sentinel*, 12 July 1998, sun-sentinel.com. Accessed 20 July 2023.

4. Friedberg et al., "Versace Murder Case Closed."

5. Yanez, "Why Was Versace a Victim?"

6. Andrew Phillips and Deborah Sharp. "Murder in Miami." *MacLean's*, 28 July 1997, vol. 110, no. 30, 23–28.

7. Deborah Ball. *House of Versace: The Untold Story of Genius, Murder, and Survival*. Crown Publishers, 2010. 189.

8. Bill Chappell. "Michael Kors Buys Italy's Versace Fashion House for $2.12 Billion." *NPR*, 25 Sept. 2018, npr.org. Accessed 20 July 2023.

9. Dena Silver. "The Versace Family Is Pretty Mad about FX's 'American Crime Story.'" *Observer*, 10 Jan. 2018, observer.com. Accessed 20 July 2023.

10. Praxilla Trabattoni and Steve Helling. "Gianni Versace's Partner Slams 'American Crime Story' Portrayal as a 'Misrepresentation.'" *People*, 29 Jan. 2018, people.com. Accessed 20 July 2023.

INDEX

aliases, 29, 40, 48, 80, 85
all-points bulletin (APB), 45
America's Most Wanted, 19, 44–45, 46, 52
Armani, Giorgio, 9, 95
Assassination of Gianni Versace, The, 97
autopsies, 27, 29, 77, 84

ballistics, 61
Barreto, Richard, 17, 21, 56, 79, 91
bloodstain pattern analysis, 37
bullet casings, 18, 27, 37–38, 41, 60–61, 69, 90

Carreira, Fernando, 64, 66–67
Casa Casuarina, 4–10, 13, 18, 45, 49, 50, 53, 66, 73, 83, 95–96
Cash on the Beach pawn shop, 51–52, 57–59, 60, 71, 73
Chicago, Illinois, 30–33, 36, 38, 44, 59, 60, 82, 83, 85, 93
Chicago Police Department, 30–33, 36, 60, 85
Chisago County, Minnesota, 28–29, 36, 83
Chisago County Attorney's Office, 36
Chisago County Sheriff's Office, 28–29
Colakovic, Mersiha, 6–8, 92
Collins Avenue, 64, 67–68
Colossus, 82
crime scenes, 26–29, 30–33, 36–38, 51, 61, 88
criminal advisories, 29–30, 33
Criss, Darren, 97
Cronin, Tom, 85
Cunanan, Andrew
- early life, 18, 19, 80, 84
- lifestyle, 21, 24, 49–50, 53, 76–77, 91
- motives, 25, 34, 70–72, 74, 76–80, 82–87, 90–93, 97
- personality, 20–21, 24, 48, 49, 79–81, 85
- relationships, 22, 24, 74, 76, 85
- search for, 18–21, 28–30, 33, 34, 36–45, 46, 48, 50–53, 54, 56–61, 63, 64, 66–70, 73, 88
- suicide, 68–70, 71, 72, 74, 91, 92

D'Amico, Antonio, 4, 7, 53, 81–82, 91, 97

East Rush Lake, 28–29, 37–38, 83

Federal Bureau of Investigation (FBI), 10, 14, 18, 20, 21, 36, 39, 40, 43–45, 46, 48, 50–51, 54, 56, 60–61, 64, 66, 77, 80, 84, 87
fingerprints, 27, 31, 36, 38, 51–52, 57, 59, 60, 69, 71, 88
Finn's Point National Cemetery, 33, 38, 83
Florida State Attorney's Office, 19
forensics, 26, 36, 37, 61, 69, 71
functional homicides, 87
FX, 97

Golden Saber bullets, 37, 90

handguns, 7–8, 30, 41, 61, 66, 68–70, 71, 83, 90, 92
Hernandez, Miriam, 48, 59
HIV and AIDS, 11, 13, 34, 54, 77, 78, 84
Holston, Ronnie, 54, 56
houseboats, 64–69, 72, 73, 88, 91

Kors, Michael, 95

Lake Como, Italy, 82
LGBTQ+ community, 11, 21, 44, 54, 56, 77, 80, 85, 91
Lincoln, Calvin, 9

Madson, David, 22, 24–29, 32, 34, 36–38, 40–42, 60–61, 66, 70, 74, 76, 83, 85–86, 88, 90, 92–93
Mafia, 10–11, 78
manhunts, 19, 36, 43–45, 48, 50, 54–63, 66, 70, 72
Metropolitan Museum of Art, 95
Miami Beach, Florida, 4–10, 14, 16–21, 45, 48–53, 54–60, 61–63, 64–71, 73, 79, 83, 88–91, 95–96
Miami Beach Police Department, 7, 9–11, 13, 14, 16–21, 52–53, 54, 56–60, 61–63, 64, 66, 67– 69, 71, 72, 79, 88, 90, 91
Miami-Dade Special Response Team (SRT), 67–68

Miglin, Lee, 30–32, 33, 36, 38–39, 40, 44, 60, 66, 83, 86–87, 90
Miglin, Marilyn, 30, 39
Milan Fashion Week, 95
Minneapolis, Minnesota, 21, 22–28, 34, 36–37, 40–42, 51, 76, 82, 83, 93
Minneapolis Police Department, 26–29, 34, 36–38, 40–42, 43, 51, 60, 93
murder weapons, 7, 27, 37–39, 41, 59, 61, 69–70, 83, 85, 87, 90
Murphy, Ryan, 97

National Center for the Analysis of Violent Crime, 84
New Jersey Police Department, 33, 43, 60
New York City Anti-Violence Project (AVP), 44, 66
News Cafe, 4, 6, 79
911 calls, 7, 28, 67
Normandy Plaza Hotel, 45, 46–50, 51–53, 59, 73, 95–96

Ocean Drive, 4, 6–8, 92
Oliva, Vivian, 51–52, 57
Orth, Maureen, 63, 96–97

pawn shop paperwork, 51–52, 53, 57–59, 60, 71, 90
Pennsville, New Jersey, 33, 40, 46, 83,
prostitution, 21, 54, 91

Reese, William, 18, 33, 38, 40, 41, 46, 48, 50, 60–61, 64, 66, 70, 71, 83, 87, 88, 90
Reineck, Torsten, 72, 91
reporters, 9–10, 56, 59, 68, 69
reward money, 66
Ryder Trauma Center, 9

Saint Patrick Catholic Church, 61–63
San Diego, California, 19, 22, 76
San Francisco, California, 22, 81–82, 91, 97
Scrimshaw, Paul, 10, 18, 78, 92
security cameras, 8, 13
serial killers, 80, 84–87, 97
South Beach, 4–10, 14
spree killers, 21, 56, 71, 72, 77, 82, 84–85, 87, 92, 96–97
stereotypes, 11, 13, 54, 56
stolen vehicles, 16–18, 21, 29, 31–33, 36, 38–39, 40, 44, 46, 48, 50, 60, 64, 71, 87, 90, 93

telephone tip lines, 43–45, 46, 50, 51, 56–57
Ten Most Wanted Fugitives list, 44, 50, 51
Thirteenth Street parking garage, 8–9, 16–18, 50, 73, 90
Tichich, Bob, 26, 40–41, 42, 87
Trail, Jeffrey, 22, 24–25, 27–28, 29, 34, 36–38, 40–42, 60, 66, 74, 76, 83, 85–87, 88, 92–93

Vanity Fair, 96
Vanover, Stephanie, 79
Vehicle Identification Number (VIN), 17–18
Versace, Donatella, 16, 91, 94–95, 97
Versace, Gianni
- early life, 7
- fashion design, 9, 10, 94–95
- funeral, 16, 61–63
- legacy, 9, 94–97
- lifestyle, 4–6, 11, 13, 21, 79–82, 85, 91
- murder, 7, 9–10, 13, 14, 18–20, 53, 54, 56–57, 60–61, 66, 70–72, 74, 77–79, 82–85, 87, 88, 90, 92, 96–97

Versace, Santo, 94
Vulgar Favors, 96–97

wanted posters, 44, 50, 54–56
warrants, 36, 59
Washington, DC, 61

ABOUT THE AUTHOR

YVETTE LaPIERRE

Yvette LaPierre lives in North Dakota with her family and teaches writing and other courses at the University of North Dakota. She writes and edits books and articles for children and adults.